Cutler's Bargain

a John Cutler mystery

by Colin Conway

Everything is negotiable.

- Salesperson mantra

Cutler's Bargain

2007

Chapter 1

"I'd like your help." Gillian Brewer rubbed her tanned upper arm as her eyes searched for something across the street.

"My help?"

Her gaze returned to me. "You do that sort of thing, don't you?" Now, she seemed unsure. She glanced at the neighboring tables and scanned the faces of their occupants. When Gillian looked at me again, she asked, "You *are* John Cutler, right?"

"Yeah, sure," I said.

She touched her sternum as if in relief. "Okay. For a second, I thought maybe I got the wrong guy."

Moments before, she'd approached my table and introduced herself. Gillian was roughly forty, a year or two older than me. Her light brown hair fell beyond her shoulders. She wore a red spaghetti-strap cotton shirt, white shorts, and sandals. A slouchy purse hung over her left shoulder. Her skin shimmered as if she'd recently applied lotion.

"May I sit?" Gillian asked. Without waiting for my answer, she dropped her purse to the ground, pulled out a chair, and sat.

We were in the outside dining area of O'Doherty's Irish Pub, and the nearby building protected us from the afternoon sun. Even in the shade, the temperature pushed into the mid-eighties. It was a comfortable August Sunday, and patrons filled every table.

Across Spokane Falls Boulevard, Riverfront Park teemed with summer activity. Kids ran through the spraying water fountain. Several small vendor booths were set up, and patrons lined them to examine their goods. At the park's edge, a guitarist with a portable amp and microphone performed a mangled rendition of the Beatles' "Help."

Gillian sat upright in her chair and looked over to the park.

"Expecting someone?" I asked.

Her eyes met mine, and she settled back into her seat. "No."

"Worried then?"

"Not really."

"Look," I said and pushed my Guinness to the side. "If this is a boyfriend thing, I'm not your guy. I've done that before, and it didn't work out so well."

"This is not about a boyfriend."

"Husband then?"

She shook her head. "It's about my business."

I rolled my lower lip down, nodded once, and pulled the beer back toward me.

A kid on a skateboard rode noisily by. The clattering of the hard rubber tires on the brick sidewalk drowned out the wailing guitarist in the park. Unfortunately, not much else could be heard. I waited until the skateboarder stopped at the corner before continuing. "What kind of business?"

"It's hard to explain."

"Because I won't understand, or because we're in public?"

Gillian opened her hands in a what-could-she-say gesture and tilted her head toward the neighbors only a few feet away.

"Start with this," I said. "Is it legal?"

She straightened, and her attention returned to the park. Her eyes narrowed as if in concentration.

Eventually, she said, "Mostly," without looking in my direction.

"Isn't that like being mostly pregnant?"

Her head turned toward me. "Does working in a gray area bother you?"

I sipped my beer. I'd done work related to sketchy things before and felt bad afterward. Those jobs more than paid the rent, but I liked feeling good about myself. The latter was a luxury and the former a necessity. Yet, I was flush due to a recent job, hence the day drinking. Luxuries were at the forefront of my thinking now.

"I prefer when things are black and white," I said.

"I'd pay you, of course."

"That's good since I don't run a charity."

Gillian's brow furrowed. "Have I offended you?"

I shook my head. "But you still haven't said what you want."

"You're a private detective."

"Who's not in his office." I saluted her with my beer. "Cut to the chase."

She leaned forward. "You were a cop. Don't look so shocked. I looked you up on the internet. It's not exactly a secret since you've been in the paper."

"I didn't say it was a secret, but what's my law enforcement history got to do with anything?"

"The gray area thing."

"You haven't said anything yet."

"I need your help."

"Most people do when they want to hire me."

Gillian glanced around once more. I wondered if this behavior was a delay tactic or something she absently did while thinking. Maybe she just liked battered renditions of classic Beatles songs. The performer now butchered "Norwegian Wood."

"Isn't it good?" I said.

Her attention returned. "Huh?"

I leaned in. "How'd you know I was here?"

She shrugged. "Maybe I followed you."

"You didn't."

"Maybe."

Could I have missed someone trailing me? I tried to remember where my head was while walking from home to the bar. I felt pretty good due to my financial position, so perhaps I had zoned out and gone into the white zone—that place where a person is completely clueless of their surroundings. I didn't think I had done that, but it was possible.

A server named Cassie approached. She smiled and pointed at my beer. "Another?"

"Not yet. Gimme a couple minutes."

Cassie thumbed over her shoulder. "It's busy in there. I'll have Alex start another." She eyed Gillian. "Get you anything?"

"Just water. I'll have something in a moment."

When Cassie left, Gillian cocked her head. "She knows you. Is this your regular place?"

The idea of zoning out bothered me. It was a good forty-five-minute walk to the bar. Being in the white zone for any portion of it was a dangerous habit to develop. "You didn't follow me," I said with certainty. "I would have seen you."

"Don't get upset." Gillian dismissively waved a hand. "I didn't follow you."

"Then why say it?"

"I don't know." She glanced at the park. "It was a joke. I'm nervous."

"No, it wasn't, and no, you aren't. Who are you looking for?"

Her head slowly turned back to me. "Maybe I got lucky and found you here."

"That didn't happen, either."

Another shrug, but this time she used a single shoulder. "I'm sorry I even said anything. Can we start over?"

"Why not come to my office?"

She stared at me for a moment, then turned toward the park again. Now, I was sure that this wasn't a delay tactic. She *was* searching for someone.

"I wanted our meeting to be in public," she said without looking at me.

"Why?" I leaned to the side to catch her attention. "You knew I was here before you ever showed up, but you didn't know what I looked like. I thought you said you looked me up on the internet."

"Your picture wasn't in the articles."

"Who told you I was here?"

She cast a sideways glance in my direction but didn't answer. It seemed she might be trying to formulate a response. I had mine ready.

"You got off on the wrong foot, lady. Not me."

Gillian turned fully back to me. "I'm sorry. I—"

I interrupted her. "I'm not sure what's with the runaround, but don't apologize. Either get with the truth or take off." I jerked my thumb toward Washington Street. "I don't need the hassle. I was having a great day until you showed up."

She remained quiet for several beats. I imagined she was deciding on a course of action. She pulled her shoulders back and defiantly lifted her chin when she did. "It's Remo."

"Remo?"

She nodded once. "That's right."

When I first arrived, I thought I saw someone standing at the edge of the park who looked like that slippery son of a bitch. It was only a momentary glimpse, but the guy I saw didn't have long hair and was dressed differently than the man I remembered. When I looked again, the guy was gone. I convinced myself it was a trick of my mind, that it was just a lookalike, and I focused on relaxing. Had I seen Remo, I would have given chase and thumped the living hell out of him.

She continued. "If you'll allow me to explain. Remo's—"

I jumped to my feet, and my chair scraped across the concrete. I leaned against the small fence that enclosed the patio and scanned every face in the park.

The patrons at the other tables anxiously watched me.

When I couldn't locate Remo, I turned to say something to Gillian, but she was also actively searching the crowded park. My face warmed, and I struggled to keep my voice calm. "Why?"

She faced me. Her voice was low and calm. "He said you would react this way."

"Of course I would. He owes me."

"He told me what happened, but trust me, Remo will make good on it."

I barked a single laugh. "He's not good for anything except lies."

"Now, c'mon. That's uncalled for. Remo's a—"

"It's been almost four months. I put my neck on the line for him. He got his money and took off. He didn't pay what we agreed to."

Gillian lifted a hand to interrupt, but my righteous indignation wouldn't let her.

I rested my hands on the metal table. It wobbled under my weight as I leaned toward her. "Remo sold me a bill of goods, and then he skipped town without paying my fee. The rumor I heard is he went to Mexico. Is that true?"

"I don't know."

My face hardened. "Maybe you think you can do the same thing? Is that what he told you to do? Get me to do some dirty work and stiff me on the fee?"

She leaned back into her chair and patted the air with her hands. "Please, Mr. Cutler, sit down."

"Guilt by association." I straightened, snapped my fingers, and angrily pointed at her. "If you're friends with that son of a bitch then we'll never work together."

"*Please*," she said. "I'll make it right."

The customers at the neighboring tables watched us with a mixture of concern and excitement. I wanted to yell at them to mind their own damn business, but I kept enough of my anger under control. I averted my eyes and peered into the crowd again.

Across the street, the guitarist stopped with his Beatles tribute and now distorted the Monkees' "Pleasant Valley Sunday." At least he got the day right.

I slowly lowered into my seat.

Gillian rested her elbows on the edge of the table. She whispered, "What if I pay what Remo owes? You know, to reset the conversation."

"When pigs fly."

"I'm serious. Remo says you're the guy to help. He was very complimentary of you, Mr. Cutler."

"Oh, I'll bet he was." I clapped and laughed with mocking glee.

I didn't care to get this woman's business. As far as I was concerned, she could fall off the face of the earth. If she took Remo with her, so much the better.

She lifted her purse into her lap. "He said you were an honorable guy."

"That's rich. Remo steals from me and then calls me honorable. Classic. A chump is what he should have called me."

"Don't hold what's happened against him. Remo's sort of a messed-up soul. He had a tough upbringing. Occasionally, he needs a guiding hand, but he's a person of goodwill."

"Goodwill?"

"I firmly believe that." She nodded.

"And you're the guiding hand?"

"Not really, no. I'm just a friend."

"But he stole from me."

She opened her purse. "Not paying one's bills is a far cry from stealing."

"I disagree."

"This is why I knew using him as a reference would cost me—especially with your history."

That gave me pause. I pulled back slightly. "*My* history? He's the one who stole." I disliked the whine in my voice, but it was too late to stop it.

"I looked you up, remember? You read like a man not to be messed with."

"Tell Remo that."

"I did." She lowered her gaze and stuck her hand into her purse.

"You're serious?"

"Of course I am."

Maybe she could hang around the earth a little bit longer. At least long enough to cover the fee that Remo ran off with.

"No checks," I said sullenly.

She nodded but kept her eyes focused on her purse. "Remo said he owed you twenty-four hundred." She glanced up. "Does that sound right?"

I was amazed. First, that Remo had told her the correct amount. And second, that I might see some of that money right now. Trying to hide my eagerness, I cleared my throat. "Yeah. Twenty-four."

"Any interest?"

I shook my head.

Gillian's eyes softened, and she smiled. It was a playful grin that bordered on a smirk. She didn't seem the type to do that to someone she had just met.

"What?" I asked.

"You should charge interest on late amounts. The banks do it. Loan sharks do it."

"You know a loan shark?"

She cocked her head, and her eyebrows lifted. "Some. Not too many, but the ones I know aren't as bad as the Hollywood reputation makes them out to be. But not charging interest on late payments shows your inexperience as a business owner."

My face hardened. "Twenty-four," I said firmly. "No interest."

"So be it." She removed her hand from the purse and rested it on the table. Underneath was a wad of folded bills. I glanced around at the other patrons on the patio, and not one looked our way. I laid my hand over Gillian's.

"Remo's debt is now mine." She pulled her hand from the table. "You don't need to count it. It's all there— interest-free."

Her smile morphed into a smirk. There was no mistaking it now. I'd misjudged her.

I dropped my hand and flipped through the bills— twenty-four Benjamin Franklins stared up. I folded them over and tucked them into my pocket.

"We could have done this at my office," I said. My gaze swept over the other patrons to ensure none had watched me count the money. As usual, they were more interested in their own lives.

"Better for this to happen in public."

"Why's that?" I looked up and followed Gillian's gaze.

Remo Lightly stood at the edge of the park next to the guitar player. He wore khaki shorts and a light blue polo shirt. His once long hair was now cut short like an aging surfer's. He looked almost respectable. Remo bent over and dropped something into the guitarist's tip bucket. The musician stopped playing to nod his appreciation.

Remo then turned and looked in our direction. When he made eye contact with Gillian, he waved like a kid coming home from summer camp. It was then he realized I sat with her. His smile vanished, and his wave slowed. It became a timid acknowledgment of my existence.

I stood abruptly, and Remo stepped backward. He faded into a crowd heading toward the carousel.

"This help you're asking for—" I pointed in the direction Remo had been. "It better not be for him."

"It's not," she said.

"Because he burnt that bridge."

She patted the air again, this time with a single hand. "I understand, but I needed to deal with Remo's debt now so it wouldn't be a thorn in our side later. In case his name came up at another time."

"A thorn." I dropped into my chair. "I could come up with better ways to describe Remo."

"I figured as much."

Cassie returned from the bar with a glass of water and a beer. She set the Guinness near my hand and the water in front of Gillian. "Have you decided yet?"

Gillian raised her eyebrows. "Would you mind if we walked for a few minutes?"

I wanted to tell her no. That the earth could start spinning again, and she could fling herself and Remo off at any time. However, the twenty-four hundred in my pocket felt good. It was money I'd written off. Maybe it wouldn't hurt to hear what she wanted.

"Will you hold the table?" I asked Cassie. "Only for a couple minutes."

"Of course."

***

We dodged a couple of cars to cross Spokane Falls Boulevard.

The guitarist now mutilated the Partridge Family's "I Think I Love You." A group of gray-haired women stood around him. They clapped and sang accompaniment. Most of the other parkgoers gave them a wide berth.

I searched for Remo as we headed toward the walking path that looped through the various sections of the park. It ran parallel with the Spokane River. I half-expected Remo to step out of the bushes and attempt an apology. If that were to happen, I'd punch him in the head. I'd waited months to do that, and the desire hadn't magically disappeared because of some cash in my pocket.

"I'm a small business owner, John. Is it okay that I call you that?"

"Call me what you like."

"Just don't call you late for dinner."

I eyed her.

Gillian waved a hand. "It's a joke my father used to say."

"Was there something you wanted to ask?"

She glanced over her shoulder and then turned completely around. She walked backward for a few steps, then turned around again. We walked side by side, and she lowered her voice. "Whatever I tell you is protected by attorney-client privilege, right?"

"I'm no attorney."

"You know what I mean."

I knew what she was after. Remo had asked me something similar when we first met but used a catholic confessional as the metaphor. Regardless, the parallel of the questions concerned me. "Whatever you say stays between us."

"Is that a law?"

"I won't be in business very long if I can't keep a secret."

Gillian stopped walking, and we faced each other. We were the only ones in that area of the asphalt trail. She glanced around before speaking.

"I own several businesses in the valley—a tanning salon, a screen printer, and a nail salon." She held up three fingers as she listed them off.

"Sounds like an active life."

"I do all right." It wasn't bragging. If anything, she sounded as if she were trying to downplay it. I appreciated that. She looked around again before speaking. "The businesses are all in the same building."

"Probably smart. Less travel time for you."

"I own the building, too. It's a three-bay retail strip. That's what I wanted at the beginning. The businesses were a bonus. They turned out to be a huge win. Maybe even more important than the building."

I reassessed her. Gillian Brewer and I were roughly the same age, but she owned a commercial building and three businesses. Not only was she an attractive woman, but she also seemed very business savvy. I had to admit that I felt slightly intimidated by her success.

Voices came from down the path. Gillian looked in their direction and gently touched my arm. "Let's walk."

I stayed in stride with her. "I'm not seeing where I come in yet."

"There's a fourth business I own." Her voice was even lower now, almost a whisper. It was hard to hear her with the ambient noise of the river and downtown traffic, let alone the waning amplification of a street musician. She said, "This one is off the books."

Remo, I thought. A woman who owned three legitimate businesses and commercial real estate wouldn't likely run across a guy like Remo. She had to be into something shady.

"What's the business?"

She fell silent as we walked. I thought it might be because she was thinking, but I noticed the voices behind us were louder now. It sounded like a group of women, and they were gaining on us. They didn't sound hostile—quite the opposite. They sounded happy. There were several laughs during their conversation.

Gillian stopped near the river's edge. "You grow up around here, John?"

"No."

She nodded a couple of times and waited for me to elaborate. When I didn't, she said, "I don't like the river at this time of year. It's always low because of the dams." Several larger rocks were visible in the middle of the water. "It's not as pretty as when the mountains have spring run-off."

A group of five older women dressed in shorts and t-shirts hurried by. None of the speed-walkers acknowledged us, and we didn't bother saying hello either. When their voices faded into the distance, Gillian said, "Let's head back."

It took two quick steps to catch up to her.

"What's this fourth business?" I asked.

"I run it from the basement of my building."

"Under the tanning joint?"

She nodded. "And the screen printer and nail salon."

"What do you do?"

"I provide a product."

My eyes narrowed. "An off-the-books product?"

"Right."

It took me a minute to suss it out.

Maybe Gillian was running a house of prostitution in the basement, but that was a service. Although, that was probably me playing word games with myself.

And she looked too damn healthy and respectable for operating a meth lab in the basement. I'd run across several labs while employed as a Seattle cop. None of those operators looked anything like Gillian. Perhaps the process had been refined in the few years I'd been away, but I doubted it.

So many ideas flitted through my mind, but I quickly discredited them. Chop shop—not in a basement. Sweatshop—not in America. Identity theft ring—it's not a product, but maybe that was a word game again. That was one to stick a pin in and come back to later.

But there was something she could be making in that basement. It was an illegal product that millions of Americans used every year in their own homes. So, that's what I guessed.

"You're growing marijuana."

Gillian anxiously glanced around as if checking to see if anyone had heard my statement. When her gaze returned to me, she said, "It should be legal."

"But it's not."

"Still. It should be. Probably will be someday."

I frowned. A couple of years ago, I ran afoul of a crew transporting bud down from Canada. Their leader was a guy on the run for a double homicide and hiding under an assumed name. People died when I found him. Tying marijuana to his actions was probably the wrong application of cause and effect. However, the drug was present in almost everything surrounding the man. The lingering impact of that experience was a deep dislike for the illegal plant.

"What are you asking me to do?"

"I hope you understand the leap of faith I'm making here. Revealing my business to you was a big step in trust."

I didn't answer.

"You don't agree?"

I stopped walking. "I'm waiting to hear what you want."

Gillian turned around, and her brow wrinkled. "You seem mad."

"I'm not mad. You're misreading what I'm feeling—it's distrust. You keep avoiding just coming out and saying what it is you want me to do."

She crossed her arms. "You said you were comfortable working in a gray area."

"That's not what I said."

"But what you did for Remo—"

"That wasn't a gray area. Remo did a job and was owed money. I helped him get paid. That's it."

"But it came from a gray area. Well, it wasn't really gray, was it? He'd committed a felony."

"He told you what he did?"

Gillian nodded.

Remo was the lookout for a heist of a payday loan business. Unfortunately, he'd allowed himself to be seen by a woman in the neighborhood. The man behind the heist refused to pay Remo. I shouldn't have gotten involved, but there was a strange charm to Remo, at least initially—a boyish nature that made me want to help him.

In the end, I peacefully resolved the issue, and Remo got his money. Then he fled town without paying me my agreed-upon fee.

I said, "Remo talks too much."

"He told me about you because I need help. Am I happy that he did the other job? No. It was stupid, but he said he was helping a friend. Am I happy that he stiffed you? No. Most certainly not. It just cost me twenty-four hundred dollars. And am I happy that he took off for several months? No. That put me in a real bind."

"But you forgave him?"

"It's Remo. I love him like a brother—a messed-up older brother, but you don't abandon family because of small screw-ups like that."

"Those don't sound like small screw-ups to me."

Gillian dismissed my concern with a wave of her hand. "As far as I'm concerned, it's a one-time thing. It won't happen again."

"You can't promise that."

She tapped her sternum. "I can."

"This thing you're asking. Is it the same thing I did for him? You want me to track down something? Someone stiffed you on a payment?"

I didn't like the idea of finding some pothead who owed her money, but it was unlikely she would pay off Remo's bill plus my fee just to square the account of some doper. It made more sense that one of her dealers ran off with a stash, and she wanted me to track it. Would I be willing to do that?

Gillian shook her head. "No one has stiffed me."

"Then what?"

"Let's walk."

I grabbed her arm and stopped her. "Enough walking. What is it you want?"

She pulled her arm free. "Please don't touch me like that."

I raised my hands. "I'm sorry, but I'm tired of the games. Tell me what's going on."

Gillian looked around for a moment, then finally announced, "I've got a leak."

"Call a plumber."

"Cute. No. That's what you would be for."

"Why do you think there's a leak?"

"Because someone broke in."

"Your grow?"

Gillian walked over to a bench near the river. She sat, and I joined her.

"They broke into the tanning salon," she said. "They gained access by throwing a cinder block through the front window."

"Maybe they were after some quick cash."

"No one breaks into a tanning salon for quick cash. They were after the grow. Trust me. Besides, they never even looked in the salon's cash register."

I turned my body and hooked one foot under the back of the opposite leg. "You have security cameras?"

"I do."

"Did you turn the footage over to the cops?"

She stared at me like I was simple.

"You can't," I said, "because then the cops would be in your building—right on top of your grow."

She touched the side of her nose and then pointed at me. "The intruders wore masks, so it wouldn't do much good to give the video to the cops, anyway. And they covered the license plate of their truck, too. Whoever these guys were, they planned ahead. I'll give them that."

"Did they bring the cinder block?"

She nodded.

"Why didn't they come through the back door? Is there one?"

"There is, but it's secured. No one is getting through there unless I want them. They came in the only way they could. They broke the window, pried open the door to the basement, then gave up."

"Why'd they do that?"

Gillian's smile was crooked. "Because there's a second door—a security door. They came unprepared for the steel. Due to that, they'll be back. I know it. They got that far only to be stopped."

"Which means they knew about your grow."

"That's what I'm saying." She opened her palm the way a magician reveals a trick. "Hence the leak."

"Just from what you've told me, a number of folks know about your grow. All your dealers. Hell, even Remo does."

"But they're professionals."

"Not Remo."

"Him, too. I know you don't have a high opinion of Remo, but trust me, he *is* a professional. And if any of the people I trust wanted to rip me off, they would have known about the second door. They would have come prepared. No, these are people from outside my circle."

She made a valid point. "Have there been any strange people coming around lately?"

Gillian waggled a hand. "Maybe, but that's hard to quantify."

I leaned in. "Explain that."

"Customers don't normally show up at my legitimate businesses."

My eyes narrowed. "Those businesses are built for walk-ins, aren't they? Maybe not the screen printing, but definitely the nails and tanning."

Gillian's smile was knowing. "Normally, those types of businesses want to attract drive-by traffic, but mine aren't. They're legitimate; don't get me wrong. They have to be, but we discourage customers. However, even though we do our best to shoo them away, people still come in. That's the problem. I can't be sure who's searching for information on the grow and who just wandered in hoping to get a tan." She shook her head. "You need to see it to understand. Will you come by and look? I'll pay for your time. Even if you say no to the job, I'll pay you to come out. What's your hourly rate?"

I glanced up and down the path. I didn't have anything going on at that moment—just some additional day drinking. But getting involved in anything related to illegal drugs wasn't something I wanted to do. I'd had that experience once, and I didn't need it again.

"I'll pass," I said.

"I'll pay double. Please, Mr. Cutler. Remo said you were the man to help. Come out and look. That's all I'm asking."

Double my regular fee sounded great, and it forced me to consider her offer, but Remo's recommendation didn't carry much weight—at least not until I talked with the man himself.

I stood and extended my hand. "It was nice meeting you. And good luck with collecting Remo's debt."

Gillian looked away briefly. When she faced me again, she stood. "And here I thought Remo was a good judge of character."

She left without accepting my hand.

Chapter 2

After paying my tab at O'Doherty's, I walked over to Monroe Street and up several blocks to a burgeoning entertainment district. Newer restaurants screamed for attention along Sprague Avenue, yet it was an aging pool hall that held the corner's prime real estate.

Several neon signs were lit in the window of Eight Ball Billiards—their effectiveness seriously diminished by the afternoon sun. I crossed the street after the light changed.

Inside, several fans blew stale air about. Overhead, The Allman Brothers Band's "Midnight Rider" played. A clacking of pool balls came from the rear of the joint.

The bartender lifted his head when I walked deeper into the establishment. He was about to holler a greeting when recognition flashed in his eyes. His face flattened, and he nodded once.

"He in the back?" I asked.

"Where else?" The bartender turned away without asking if I wanted anything. I couldn't blame him. I'd long given up the pretense of drinking there.

A young black male stood at the edge of the pool table area. He leaned against the pony wall that separated the section from the traditional bar. The kid couldn't have been more than sixteen. He eyed me with open hostility.

I passed a couple of pool tables before stopping to wait. The fat man I wanted to speak with sat on an extended bench near the back wall. He was conversing with another young black male I knew—Tremaine.

Most of the tables were occupied. A young Asian couple smiled and laughed at the first table. It must have been a date as the woman giggled more than she needed to, and the guy explained more than he should.

For the next few tables, solo sharks practiced their skills. None of them talked nor looked at the others. Although it was evident that they scoped out the competition by the amount of side-eye flashed as each moved about their respective tables.

No one played on the furthest table.

From a shadow in the far corner, a thick-shouldered male approached. He wore a black tank-top, khaki cargo shorts, and running shoes with no socks. His well-defined arms were free of tattoos. He sidled up to me to watch the sharks.

"Hey, John."

"Keith."

Neither of us looked at the other, and we kept our voices low.

He asked, "How's it been?"

"Good. You?"

"Same, same."

I didn't look at the man I was waiting for. Instead, my gaze drifted back toward the teenager holding up the pony wall. When he caught me looking, my eyes flicked to the giggling young woman at the first table.

"He send you over?" I asked Keith. "I didn't see a signal."

Now, Keith leaned forward. His attention seemed to be on the bartender, but he didn't care what was going on over there any more than I did. "He's sick."

My eyes caught Keith's. "Like a cold?"

"The terminal kind."

I remained silent and watched the young woman again. She missed an easy shot that I suspected was on purpose. Her date made a big show of telling her it was all right and to try the shot again.

"Don't bring up how he looks," Keith said. "Just handle your business, then be on your way."

"Understood." My gaze flicked to the young man at the edge of the pool area. He intently watched the fat man and Tremaine.

"Who's the kid?"

"Dontari. Tremaine's brother."

I eyed Keith. "I didn't know he had a brother."

"Dontari's not allowed to come back here. The kid's a loose cannon."

Without letting me ask why, Keith smiled like we were old friends and patted my back. He motioned in a friendly manner toward one of the sharks, then returned to his corner in the shadow.

Overhead, The Guess Who's "These Eyes" started.

There was movement near the back wall, and Tremaine headed toward me.

I lifted my chin in greeting. "Hey, man. How are—"

He walked by without so much as a nod.

I fought the desire to grumble, "What's your problem?" but kept my mouth shut. I tracked him until he met with his brother. The two left the bar.

When I turned toward the back, the fat man motioned for me to join him. Deacon Hogue sat alone on the bench with a pool cue clutched in his right hand. In front of him sat his table—only he and his guests played on it. I'm not sure what his relationship was with the pool hall owners. I'd never been able to ascertain it, but I'd never tried very hard, either. Hell, I'd only recently learned his last name. There were certain things I accepted in life simply on faith. Two of those things were that this table belonged to Deacon, and this bench was where he conducted business.

It had only been a few weeks since I last saw him—maybe a month—he'd lost weight since then. The first time I noticed any weight loss was in the spring. Over the summer, I thought maybe he was on some sort of fad diet.

When a morbidly obese man loses weight, it's hard to notice it initially. There was no mistaking it now that Keith pointed it out. I wondered how long Deacon had been this way.

It was difficult to tell the color of his skin in the low light, but his usually sweaty forehead was dry. He wore an oversized t-shirt that hung loosely from his shoulders. His polyester slacks appeared baggy, but the man was sitting. It might have been an illusion of the low light.

Would I have picked up on him being sick without Keith's help, or would I have continued to think that his diet was slowly working wonders?

"Cutler," Deacon said. "What are we trading today?"

"Remo Lightly."

Deacon's face soured as if he'd just sucked on a lemon. "That's a name that hasn't been uttered in a few months."

"He's back in town."

He raised an eyebrow. Deacon didn't know many drug dealers in town, but Remo was a special case. For starters, he'd been in the game for decades. Most guys quit in their twenties, tired of being targeted by law enforcement, and in constant danger of either jail or the cemetery. Those that get out tend to grow up and take legitimate jobs.

Remo Lightly had been born under a lucky star. When he was younger, he sold to high school kids who lived on the South Hill. Now those kids had matured into respectable citizens who still lived on that posh side of town. They'd grown comfortable and dependent on buying their weed from Remo. This provided him with low-key, life-long clientele.

The second reason Deacon knew about Remo was that I shared the story of him running off with my fee. The fat man found it a funny story at the time. He even asked me to retell it about a month after it happened so he could laugh at it again.

"I'm serious," I said. "I just saw him."

Deacon appraised me. "And the man is still walking?"

I nodded.

"You must be in a good mood, or he made good on his debt."

I patted my pocket.

"What happened? Remo developed a case of the guilts and came home to make good?"

"No, a woman happened."

Deacon waggled his pool cue. "Well, well. Remo's got himself a monied woman. Will wonders never cease?"

"It's not that type of relationship."

"Then what is it?"

"Business. She wants to hire me and brought his account current in a show of good faith."

Deacon lowered his chin. "The woman did that to avoid hard feelings?" Now, he eyed me. "Why would she do such a thing?"

"Because Remo referred me."

"Why would she even mention the man? She could have saved herself the scratch by keeping her mouth closed. You think she's the type of woman not to keep a secret?"

"I don't think that."

Deacon rested his head against the wall. "You take the job?"

"No. Remo's referral put me off." I didn't mention the connection to marijuana. Deacon didn't have the same issues with illegal drugs as I did. As far as he was concerned, it was simply a product that folks traded. But Gillian's secret still needed to be maintained.

"A woman with enough money to make good on Remo's debt might have been useful. What did she want you to do?"

"We never got that far."

He bumped my elbow with his. "So you took the money and ran. Now, you're learning." He realized something and turned to me. "But you came here to talk about Remo."

"I want to find him."

"Why? Why would you want such a thing after his debt has been cleared? Even you aren't angry enough to knock around a man after he's paid up."

I held up an open palm. "If someone handed you a wad of cash, wouldn't you want to know a little more before you started believing it was yours?"

"You know what they say about gift horses, Cutler."

"I also know what they say about looking before you leap."

"Good point." Deacon rotated his pool cue in wider circles now. His eyes narrowed as he thought. "Where could you find Remo? Where could you go?"

I turned to watch some of the sharks playing. My attention scanned the pool area. Only Keith stood in the darkness. Typically, Deacon had two men watching over him. Had his sickness cost him a confidante?

"There is a man named the Turk," Deacon announced with finality. "Talk with him. He might know where to find someone like Remo."

I didn't bother to hide my displeasure. "Anyone else?"

"You know him?"

"I do."

"I'm sure there are others who might give you a line on Remo, but there's no one else that I can point you to. You can always skip the Turk and let this whole Remo thing slide. Just be a citizen and enjoy the money in your pocket."

My face pinched.

"But that's not the John Cutler way, is it?"

"Why the Turk?"

"Because he and Remo run in the same circles. The Turk is smarter, though. He's got aspirations."

"You sure they're not delusions?"

"Trust me, John. There's more going on with the Turk than you give him credit for. Someday he's going to do more than sling dope. You watch."

I found that hard to believe. "Where can I find him?"

Deacon cocked his head. "Last I heard, he's renting a place on Pacific, east of Division. It's an old apple warehouse. Supposedly, he converted the third floor into an apartment. It's the building with the painted logo on the side. You know the one I'm talking about?"

"Got an address?"

"Do I look like Google? Besides, I just told you where he's at."

I nodded my thanks.

"Now, I need you to do for me."

That's how it was with Deacon—favor for favor.

"What?" I asked.

"Tremaine."

I looked toward the front of the bar where the young man had exited with his brother only a few minutes prior. "What about him?"

"He's getting in deep with the Dead Boys."

"Nothing I can do about that. If he's in with a gang, they're not going to let him out because I give him some encouraging words. That's not how it works."

Deacon frowned.

"Yeah, okay. What's his brother got to do with this?"

His tongue poked the inside of his mouth and then made its way around the front of his teeth. Finally, his lips parted, and he said, "Dontari." It was said with exasperation. "He's the one who got Tremaine into this mess."

"He looks younger."

"So he is, but that doesn't mean Tremaine isn't protecting him by getting involved."

"They aren't wearing any colors."

The fat man smirked. "The Dead Boys don't wear colors. They want to be like spies and fit in with any neighborhood they're in. Before anyone knows they've arrived, the war is already over."

I watched the nearest pool shark make a difficult shot. "What is it you're asking?"

"Tremaine's mother is worried."

Deacon and Rosemary had a relationship that they carried on for years. I don't think it was anything more than platonic, but Deacon held those cards close to the vest.

I asked, "What do you think about it?"

"If Tremaine wants to help his brother," he said remorsefully, "he's a grown man."

I wasn't sure that Tremaine was even eighteen yet, but that's how the world worked down here. While the rest of the world now wanted to categorize twenty-somethings as children, those living close to the street were supposed to be adults quicker than need be.

Deacon lowered his head. "If this is his path, Tremaine needs to walk it smart." He looked up. "That's why I want you to talk with him."

"Because I know so much about gangs?"

"Because you were a cop, John. You can tell him things."

"He might not like what I say."

Deacon's face flattened. "Don't talk down to him like a cop. Don't scold him like a father. Talk to him like you lived down here. You once did, remember?"

"I don't live too far even now."

"That's why I want you to do this. Speak with him. Will you do that? For me?"

I leaned my head against the wall and stared at the quiet pool table in front of us. "Where can I find him?"

Deacon reached into a pocket and pulled out a piece of paper. I opened it and saw a name, address, and phone number. "He's expecting a call from you, but he's not happy about it."

"What about Dontari?"

"What about him?"

"You want me to talk with him, too?"

Deacon stared at me. He seemed to be formulating a response. His eyes narrowed then he looked away. "There's a rabbit in *Bambi*—"

"Thumper," I said. I'd watched the movie with my daughter. I was surprised that Deacon could even pull the reference. As far as I knew, the man didn't have any kids.

"Right. Thumper. He said don't say anything if you can't say something nice." Deacon eyed me. "In respect to Tremaine's mother, I'm gonna hold my tongue about her youngest son."

"I hear you."

"So, talk with Tremaine." He leaned forward and stood with some effort. "I'm gonna practice now. Good luck, John."

***

I could have walked back to my home office in West Central and collected my truck, but that was a forty-five-minute walk. Heading to the Turk's new apartment was roughly twenty minutes. It would make my walk home even longer, but it seemed the wiser course of action.

Yaban Karga was a drug dealer. I didn't know if he was genuinely Turkish, but he looked like he might have been. I'd met him while bouncing at Club Royale—the hottest nightclub in the city. That's not saying much. Spokane isn't New York or Los Angeles. Its club scene isn't even close to Seattle. There was Club Royale, the Double Dribble, and Crazy 8's.

The Turk was attracted to Club Royale because it had the current 'it factor.' Since everyone wanted to get in—the waiting line proved it—Karga wanted to be there to sell his product.

I found the warehouse that Deacon described. On the west brick wall was a faded logo for Stanley Apples. Several pieces of fruit tumbled out of a wooden crate. Under the logo was the tagline *An Apple a Day*. That was it. There didn't seem to be anything missing. Marketing was simpler back then and less in your face.

According to Deacon, Karga lived on the third floor in a converted apartment. I walked around the building and found two entrance doors. Both were locked, and no one answered either after my knocking. I returned to the front of the building.

I recalled my first meeting with Karga.

Club Royale's owner didn't want drugs sold inside his club. If they were used discretely, that was another thing entirely. Bosco liked capitalism. It's why he fled here after the collapse of the USSR. But he also knew the power of the state. He'd happily flaunt certain rules while strictly adhering to others. Bosco's business was keeping people inebriated. The competition of illegal painkillers cut into his profit, and the federal government frowned upon anyone providing aid to those participating in the distribution. Therefore, Bosco straddled a line when dealing with Yaban Karga.

My options for finding the Turk today were limited. I could hang out in front of his building all afternoon, but the guy might never return. Maybe he was even out of town. Perhaps he'd taken a vacation.

And if I could somehow locate his phone number, Karga didn't seem the type to accept a call from a stranger. I'd have had to leave a message and provide some compelling reason for him to call me back. Maybe I could have devised a clever ruse, but I didn't feel like trying.

I figured I'd wait a couple of minutes longer. I turned and studied the building again. It didn't reveal any new secrets that it hadn't shown moments before.

My thoughts returned to Karga.

We caught the Turk dealing in a Club Royale VIP room one night. I immediately tossed Karga out of the club. We didn't call the cops because we preferred to deal with things in our own way. All things considered, we handled Karga with kid gloves. That's because Bosco wanted him back inside the club—just not his drugs. If we sent Karga to the Double Dribble or Crazy 8's, the college girls he tended to attract would follow him there. It was better if they all danced and drank at Club Royale than those north side bars. If a little something was sold outside the club, we couldn't stop that. A patron discreetly snorting or swallowing something while inside was okay so long as we didn't know. It was all about plausible deniability when it came to the cops and the liquor board. If they couldn't prove it happened inside our establishment, then it never happened.

With a final glance at the former Stanley Apples warehouse, I shook my head. It was time to go. I had walked half a block east toward Division Street when I saw him turn a corner. I stopped and waited.

Yaban Karga strutted along the sidewalk. It wasn't at a fast pace, though. Instead, it was the parade of a peacock. Two teenage girls excitedly stuttered and skipped in his wake.

The Turk's arms swung wide with each step. He wore a white tank-top, green sweatpants, and bright white Adidas. His Kangol hat was kicked back on his head. He looked like the star of his own rap video.

Both teenagers wore white shorts and black Nirvana t-shirts. They seemed too young to have ever listened to Kurt Cobain. They both wore flip-flops.

The Turk slowed when he neared. He glanced back at the girls, then faced me. "Yes?"

"Where can I find Remo?"

His eyes narrowed. "I know you."

"We've met."

Karga repeatedly pointed at me. "The club." He snapped his fingers. "You are the bouncer, the one who threw me out."

The girls giggled, and Karga angrily shushed them. They quieted and eyed each other like scolded children.

"I don't work there anymore," I said.

"Then why should I help you? You no longer serve a purpose. Maybe I should treat you the way you treated me?"

I studied the girls. The dark-haired one looked away. The girl with blond hair stared defiantly at me.

"How old are you?" I asked.

Karga held out his hand to block my view of them. "None of your business is how old they are. You have nothing they want."

The girls giggled again and leaned into each other. They whispered amongst themselves.

"Go on," Karga said to me. He dismissively waved his hand. "Leave us."

"What if I call the cops? How about I tell them what you've got going on here."

Karga shrugged. "What do I care what you tell them? We are not doing anything wrong." He looked at the girls, then motioned toward me. "Tell him. Are we doing something wrong?"

The girl with blond hair said, "Not yet." She playfully bumped her shoulder into her friend's. They huddled with laughter. The Turk shushed them again.

"Where's Remo?" I asked.

"Five hundred." He held up as many fingers. "And I will tell you."

"I'm not paying you five hundred for anything."

He glared at me. Karga didn't seem the type to negotiate against himself, so I said, "Fifty." The twenty-four hundred in my pocket was making me feel more than generous.

"Three hundred." Karga looked at the girls and smiled.

"For what?"

"The girls are going to have a party, and you need to cover their cost."

My brow furrowed. "I'm not paying for them to do your drugs."

"Then come do some with them." He gestured toward the teenagers. "There is more than enough to go around, but you will pay."

"No."

He smirked. "Have it your way, bouncer man. Go home and play with yourself."

The girls openly laughed now. The Turk stepped toward the front door and joined in their frivolity. His chuckling pissed me off.

Maybe I could have grabbed Karga and slugged the information out of him, but two witnesses were standing by. I could imagine the young women testifying to what they saw. Haggling still seemed my wisest course of action.

"One hundred," I said.

Karga stopped fiddling with the lock. His eyes brightened with the continued negotiation. "That is barely enough for a real party. Two hundred."

"One hundred is more than enough for what you've got planned." For added emphasis, I said, "And it's all I got on me."

The Turk considered my words for a moment, then he looked me up and down. His lips pursed, and he noisily sucked air between his teeth. Finally, he pointed at the blond girl and then motioned to me. "Liliya, get his money."

I pulled the wad of cash from my pocket.

Karga's eyes widened. "You lied! You could have afforded the five hundred."

"Consider it a tax," I said as I peeled off a single Benjamin. "I feel bad contributing to the delinquency of minors."

Liliya snatched the hundred from my fingers. "I'm old enough," she said. "Like you'll ever know." She balled the bill into her fist and joined Karga. The other girl quickly joined them.

I shoved the money back into my pocket.

"I don't feel good helping a liar," the Turk said.

"I could have easily beat the truth out of you."

Karga's eyes narrowed. "Not with them standing here."

"Those two wouldn't have stopped me."

He looked briefly away. When his gaze returned, it swept past me to the teenagers. "Remo—that's what this is about. Not me." It sounded like he was convincing them of what he was about to do.

"That's right," I said. "This is about Remo. There's no confusion."

Karga relaxed. "You see. I've done nothing wrong." Irritation flashed in his eyes when he turned toward me. "This is still worth more than one hundred dollars."

"Just tell him, Yaban," Liliya said. She impatiently moved toward the door, and her hand rested on the knob.

"Yeah," the brunette friend chimed in. "We don't have all day."

"Fine," the Turk said with a petulant nod. He crossed his arms and jutted his chin out. "It is best to try The Well. Remo's sister is the owner."

"What's her name?"

"What do I look like? The Google?"

I balled a fist and stepped toward him.

Karga lifted his hands in defense. "Elva! Her name is Elva."

****

The Well lurked at the corner of Washington Street and Second Avenue like an old man asking for spare change. It was a squat building with a blue awning and white flaking paint. It made no bones about what it was or who it served.

Inside, soft music played in the background. It took me a moment to pick it up, but it sounded like a disco song that I'd heard before. I couldn't immediately place it, but I didn't try too hard either. It was disco, after all.

The bar stunk of cigarettes. A couple of years prior, the state banned smoking in all establishments. Any place with history still smelled of cigarettes. I'd recently given up smoking, so the aroma bothered me. Not in a prissy way, but in the way someone misses the touch of an old lover—even when that person was terrible for them.

I approached the bar and sat on a stool.

A bartender walked over. Her stringy, salt and pepper hair fell to her shoulders. I tried to make out her age, but her skin seemed weathered prematurely and grayish. She was probably in her fifties and had worked in bars her entire adult life. She wore a yellow t-shirt with a photo of a reared-up bear and the tagline *Quit Yer Bitchin'*.

"What're you having?" she asked.

"Elva Lightly?"

She briefly mashed her lips together. "We got beer or liquor. No wine. If you want the good stuff, go down the street."

"Gimme a beer."

The bartender turned to a cooler and grabbed a Pabst. She snapped open the can and thunked it on the counter. Beer foamed through the opening. "Two bucks."

I pulled a twenty from my pocket and laid it on the bar. She snatched it and walked off to make change. She took her time doing so.

I sipped my beer and listened to the music. The disco song faded and was replaced by that tune about drinking pina coladas and getting caught in the rain. My mother listened to it with her friends when I was young. That was back when she still enjoyed music, and I still cared enough to pay attention to what she liked. I didn't know who sang it or if the guy ever had another hit.

Only a few folks were in the bar, and their heads were down as they went about their business. It was a stark contrast to what was occurring over at O'Doherty's. That place had a festive atmosphere—people were enjoying their afternoon. It seemed The Well's patrons were simply killing their day. To them, drinking was an act of survival.

The bartender returned and laid the change on the counter. "Why're you asking about me?"

"If you're Elva Lightly, I'm looking for your brother."

She rolled her eyes. "Oh, Christ. What's Remo done this time?"

"He's back in town."

"For like a minute. What'd he do now?"

"He owed me money."

Elva's brow furrowed. "Owed? He made good?"

"Someone covered his debt."

"No shit." She whistled softly. "So, you're not looking to hurt him?"

"Not anymore." It seemed Elva had trouble comprehending those words, so I added, "Why? Is someone else looking to hurt him?"

She shrugged. "Who knows with Remo? One moment his life is going great. The next, not so much. He's like a roller coaster. No. He's like a pinata, and everyone wants a turn with the stick."

"I only want to ask him some questions."

"About?"

"The person who made good on his debt."

"Yeah?" Elva said. "I'd like to know about that, too. Who was it?"

I sipped my beer and watched her.

She leaned a hip against the back bar. She crossed her arms and studied me. "You promise you ain't about to hurt him?"

"Cross my heart."

Her eyebrows lifted. "And hope to die?"

"Not for Remo."

"I wouldn't think so." She looked out the window. "Let me think about it."

Elva walked off to help another customer.

I sipped my beer and listened to the music. Another seventies tune came on. I couldn't place this one, but I knew I'd heard it before. The lyrics didn't come easily, and the chorus was muddled. My childhood was filled with music. My mom had been more carefree back then. Uncle Reuben was alive, too. She played rock & roll and folk music. Reuben spun funk and soul on his record player. I liked his music better.

After a few songs I recognized, I finished my beer. I shook the empty can and pushed it away.

Elva returned then. "Another?"

"Going to tell me where to find Remo?"

Her eyes flicked to the empty can.

"Sure," I said.

If she wasn't going to extort me for the information, the least I could do was order another beer. She pulled a can from the cooler and snapped it open. After she set it gently on the bar, she slipped all the bills from the counter. "For my tip."

So, she was coercing me, but in a nicer way than I'd ever experienced.

I pulled the beer toward me and waited.

"Let me see your driver's license," she said.

"What for?"

"If anything happens to Remo, I want to know where to point the cops."

Reluctantly, I pulled my wallet out and removed the driver's license. I hadn't planned on hurting Remo—maybe a little roughing up. He deserved as much. I tossed the ID on the counter.

Elva grabbed a pad of paper and a pen. She jotted my name and address down. When she finished, she pushed the card back to me. Then she turned the page and wrote something else. She tore the second page out and laid it on the hardwood. Elva tossed the pad under the bar.

I looked at what she'd given me—it was an address on Dean Avenue.

"That's my place," she said.

"Is a man home?"

"Besides Remo? No. Why? You hoping we could hook up?"

That left me speechless.

Elva smirked. "I haven't had a steady man in years. And you don't need to go into my place, anyway. Remo stays in the apartment above the garage. Entrance is around the side. It's easy to find."

I slipped off the stool.

"If you feel like mixing it up with him, don't tear up the apartment. I spent some money making it nice, and I know where you live now."

I raised a hand like I was swearing in before a judge. "I only want to talk with your brother."

"Well, that's good. Make sure it stays that way."

Chapter 3

It took forty minutes to walk to Elva Lightly's house. My plans for an afternoon of day drinking had been replaced by hours of walking. I wasn't upset either way. The wad of cash in my pocket was a pleasant reminder of why I was on this goose chase.

Elva's home sat at the corner of Dean Avenue and Belt Street. It was a two-story affair that seemed to have been taken care of. The house was dark blue with bright white trim. A lush green lawn appeared freshly cut. There weren't any flowers or shrubs for her to fuss with—a low-maintenance yard for a woman who worked her own business. It appeared that serving drinks to the downtrodden had been good to her. She wasn't living in a mansion, but she wasn't about to sleep under a bridge.

The house stood out amongst its neighbors. Many were not taken care of so lovingly, and the ones that were had lawns adorned with flowers and shrubbery. There were a couple of For Sale signs on her block. The real estate market had been hot nationwide, and folks were buying cheap homes to flip them. However, that crazy behavior hadn't yet come to the Zone—the derogatory name for Elva's neighborhood.

A three-foot-tall chain-link fence ran around the yard. There was a double-swing gate that blocked the entrance to the driveway. I opened it and stepped through.

Set back from the house was a two-story garage. It was painted in the same blue with white highlights.

If Remo wasn't there, I was only a half-mile from my place. I would head home and grab my truck. After that, the search for Remo would speed up immensely.

Was this a fool's errand? Should I even care why Gillian Brewer wanted to hire me? If I didn't want to work for her, asking Remo about her shouldn't make any significant difference. Maybe I did want to work with the woman. A job with a double fee certainly was intriguing, but there was something more.

It wasn't the woman—I knew that. First, I wasn't foolish enough to believe I was a knight in shining armor who had to save every damsel in distress. That lesson had already been taught to me.

Second, she wasn't a helpless princess. The woman was far more intelligent than I was. She'd bought commercial real estate, started several businesses, and ran some sort of illegal enterprise. It took me a week to prepare a simple tax return for a one-man private detective agency.

Then what was it that made me want to help?

I immediately thought of her intelligence. Could it be so simple? Did I want to feel superior to her somehow? I shook my head. My inability to evolve was showing. Did other men worry about the same bullshit that I did? Or did they blissfully travel through life, unaware that their opinions and feet were still stuck in the primordial soup?

A curtain moved slightly in a window above the garage. My gaze snapped to it, and the fabric dropped back into place.

I hurried up the driveway and stepped through another short gate connecting the garage to the house. The backyard, a small concrete patio, and a stairwell to the second-story apartment were on the other side.

The door opened at the top of the stairs, and Remo Lightly's head popped out.

"Remo," I called.

He immediately ducked back inside, and the door slammed.

I hurried up the stairs, taking them two at a time. When I arrived at the top, I banged on the door.

"Remo, you son of a bitch, open up!"

Inside, footfalls hurried back and forth.

I banged on the door again. "Remo! Stop screwing around."

A window slid noisily open at the rear of the building.

I tried the doorknob, futilely twisting it, but it remained locked. "Shit." After clomping down the stairs two at a time, I raced around the back of the garage.

Remo Lightly hung from the second-story apartment's rear window. It was a smaller one, like it belonged in a bathroom. Remo's arms were fully extended, and his head moved left and right to get a better view of the ground below him. When he saw me, his eyes widened.

"Let go," I said, "and fall down."

His feet scrambled for purchase against the side of the garage as he tried to climb back into the window. Remo's biceps flexed while he desperately tried to pull himself up. He wasn't naturally athletic, so getting momentum in that direction took considerable effort. It astonished me that he was able to hang on for that long.

I stepped forward, jumped up, and grabbed an ankle. When my body returned to the earth, Remo came with me.

"Ah!" he cried as he fell.

When his feet hit the lawn, Remo squeaked and collapsed into a heap. He immediately curled into a tight ball. He wrapped his arms around his knees and tucked his chin to his chest. Remo closed his eyes and hollered, "Don't hit me!"

"I'm not going to hit you."

"Don't hit me!" he screamed.

"I'm not going—"

"Don't hit me!"

"Shut up, dummy." I kicked him in the tail bone.

Remo bounced away and looked up in shock. "What'd you do that for?"

"Because you're shouting like an idiot."

He flopped onto his back and rested on his elbows. "You're really not going to hit me?"

"Gillian paid off your debt."

"She told me she might."

"We're square."

His brow furrowed. "Then why are you here?"

"I've got some questions."

"About?"

"You and Gillian." I glanced around. No neighbors watched us, but I didn't like the optics of me standing over Remo, especially after him screaming for me not to hit him. "Get up. Let's go inside."

"You sure you're not going to hit me?"

"Remo, if you keep asking, I'm gonna start thinking maybe I should."

He hurriedly got to his feet. "Hey, now." He lifted two fingers in the victory sign. "Peace, man. Way better than war. Am I right? Maybe we should go inside and get outta the sun?"

"That's what I was suggesting." I motioned him toward the stairs.

He took a step and jumped in pain. He hopped around on one foot. "My ankle. I think I sprained it." Remo grasped it with a hand. "When I fell."

"You shouldn't jump out windows."

"I didn't jump. You pulled me."

I pushed him, and his weight fell onto the twisted ankle.

He howled, "Oh!"

"Stop crying." I pushed him again. "Up the stairs."

Remo hopped his way up to his apartment. "You don't have to be so rough."

"And you didn't have to run off with my fee."

He paused at his door. "Are you still mad about that?"

"No, I've let it go."

Remo unlocked the door. "That's good to hear. I was thinking maybe—"

I shoved him inside. Remo stumbled forward until he fell into a recliner. The footrest snapped up into place. He instinctively grabbed his ankle and moaned.

The apartment was decorated in the manner an older woman's might be. There was a short couch, two small recliners, and a wooden coffee table. In the corner of the living room was a glass hutch. Inside were antiques like old Zippo lighters, vintage military insignia, and ceramic bells.

"Can you believe all this stuff?" Remo said. His voice was strained from the pain in his ankle.

"Where'd it come from?"

"My grandparents' house. Everything in here is." He waved a hand about. "Elva salvaged it all so she could furnish the place after she built it out."

I faced Remo, and he straightened.

He said, "But you didn't come here to talk about antiques."

"Why'd you run off with my fee, Remo?"

"Oh, geez, Cutler. I just got crazy when I saw the money."

"It wasn't that much."

Remo leaned forward. "But it should have been all mine."

"You screwed up the job, Remo. Then you made things worse by running off with my half."

He flopped back into the chair. "I know."

I studied him. The last time I'd seen him, he looked like an aging pothead. Now, he looked sort of respectable—like a graying teacher on their summer break.

"You shaved your mustache," I said.

Remo's fingers danced along his upper lip. "Yeah."

"Afraid I was going to find you?"

"No." He scoffed. "I met a girl."

"In Mexico?"

"Yeah. She didn't like the caterpillar." His face brightened briefly then he realized it might be a bad idea to look happy. "You didn't come here to talk about my facial hair either."

"How do you know Gillian?"

Remo reached for his ankle. "You didn't have to yank me outta the window."

"Why were you running?"

He rolled his eyes. "I got scared."

"We're straight, Remo. Gillian took care of it. I want to know why she'd do such a thing."

"Me and Gillian, we go back a ways."

"How far?"

"A few years."

I sat on the arm of the small couch. "She doesn't seem like a woman to be messed up in the drug business. She seems like a South Hill soccer mom—"

Remo laughed. "She doesn't have kids. She had a husband before, but never any rug rats. Dodged that bullet if you ask me."

"My point is she doesn't seem the type of woman to be growing dope. And definitely not the type to be running with the likes of you."

"Hey, that's uncalled for." Remo was about to say something further, but he moved his leg and grimaced.

When his face returned to normal, he reconsidered me and shrugged. "Whatever."

"How'd you guys meet?"

"High school."

Remo was in his mid-to-late forties. "Unless you failed several grades, there's no way you went to school with her."

"No, man. She was *in* school. I sold weed *at* the school."

"Ah, now I get it. That was more than a few years ago."

"Tell me about it." His gaze took on a wistfulness. "You know, I tried to hook up with Gillian back then. Yeah, for real."

"I don't need to know that."

He rubbed his ankle and continued down memory lane. "Man, she was pretty. I mean, she's pretty now, but she was super cute back then. A real heartbreaker. But she wasn't having any of the ol' Remo charm. And believe you me, I had some charm back then. It wasn't just the dope getting the ladies."

"Remo."

"Okay, maybe some of her friends." He snickered to himself. "They were pretty gullible when it came to the smoke. Gillian didn't fall for it, though. She was always a smart cookie."

That threw me. "Cookie?"

Remo's eyes regained their focus, and he grunted. He angrily waved a hand. "It's this furniture, man. Makes me talk like my grandmother."

"High school for her was more than twenty years ago."

"Yeah. So? You got a problem with that?"

"Now, she's growing, and you're selling again."

Remo winced as he rubbed his ankle. "I never stopped selling, man. Oh, maybe for a minute, so I could try the regular job thing. Worked at McDonald's and one of those rent-to-own furniture joints. Both sucked the big one. You get what I'm saying? I tried swinging a hammer and almost lost a thumb. I'll never do that again. So, I stuck with the one thing I was good at."

"How'd you end up working with Gillian?"

"I traded up as they say."

"Why?"

He shrugged. "She promised a better cut."

"How so?"

Remo studied his ankle. "Gillian removed the middleman. She's the grower, see? And I get my product directly from her. Usually, there's somebody in the middle."

"The middleman."

"You get it." Remo nodded. "But now there's no one, so she gave me a better split. Who wouldn't want to work with her?"

"How long has this deal with Gillian been going on?"

"About a year." He frowned. "Except for that time, I went down to Mexico."

"When you stole my fee."

He sighed. "Yeah. She wasn't very happy about that. I can't say as I blame her."

"I wasn't very happy about that, either."

His eyes narrowed. "Well, no. I guess not."

I cocked my head. "You were working with her when you got involved with Double G?"

"What's wrong with that? A guy can't work two jobs?"

Double G ran a small crew that pulled heists and insurance scams. He'd occasionally bring in other guys to help. Remo was brought in on the recommendation of a friend. After Remo screwed up, Double G ostracized both men. They were lucky that's the worst they got.

"When did you tell Gillian about the second job?"

Remo shrugged. "When I got back from Mexico. I mean, they don't run in the same circles. He didn't need to know about her either."

"So, she doesn't know it was Double G?"

"I don't want to worry her."

"And he doesn't know about her?"

Remo's eyes widened. "Oh, no. That would be like waving red meat in front of a tiger."

I rested an elbow on my knee. "Why'd you do it, Remo? Why get involved with Double G?"

"I told you before—it sounded like a safe job with easy money."

"You said that *before* you ran off with my fee. I think maybe you owe me a different truth now."

Remo stared at me. "Double G's got his fingers in everything, man. The way I figured it, if I helped him, maybe he would owe me one. You know, like down the road or something."

"If he paid you at the end of the job, then he wouldn't have owed you anything at all."

"But he didn't pay," he whined. "He stiffed me."

"Just like you stiffed me."

Remo's shoulders slumped. "But you wanted half."

"Half of something is better than a hundred percent of nothing, which is what you would have gotten if I hadn't helped."

He petulantly shook his head. "Still. The whole thing wasn't right."

"You screwed up, Remo."

"Not that bad."

"You didn't know that until I figured it out. Then you ran off with my fee. He screwed you for screwing up, so you screwed me, but I was the one who did his job right."

Remo threw his hands in the air. "I know, I know. How many times do I have to say it?"

"And you never returned any of my calls, Remo. What the hell?"

He appeared contrite. "I got rid of my phone because I thought you might be able to track me."

"Do I look like the FBI?"

"You're still mad even after Gillian paid?"

I thought about the money in my pocket. "I'll get over it, although you owe her now."

Remo nodded. "I'll make it up to her, man. I'm good at what I do."

"Is that why she paid your debt?"

"I'd like to think it was because she likes me, but let's be honest, it's because of my clients."

"Like you said, she's a smart cookie."

He frowned. "This furniture."

"Tell me what you know about her problem."

"She didn't tell you?"

I shook my head. "She wants me to come out to her place and check it out. All she said was that she had a leak."

"That's what she's thinking."

"You told her I could help. Are you thinking if I can, maybe she'll owe you one? Like Double G was supposed to?"

"No, man. That's not it." Remo pushed down on the footrest. It snapped into place, and the chair righted itself. He seemed to have forgotten about his ankle. "Someone is onto her, and she can't turn to the cops."

"How is someone onto her?"

"How would I know? I'm not the detective. You are."

"She said no one comes by to get a tan."

Remo laughed. "You don't get it."

I watched him.

"You need to see the place like she said. Then you'll understand what's going on."

"Who do you think is talking?"

Remo's eyes widened. "Not me." Now, he touched his chest with both hands. "I know better than to talk. Trust me. I avoid trouble by keeping my mouth shut around anyone who even smells like pork."

"What about Double G?"

He seemed offended now and pulled back. "You think he's part of this?"

"How would I know? I'm wondering who you might have talked to."

Remo jumped to his feet in indignation, but his right ankle gave out, and he stumbled in that direction. He pirouetted twice, then hopped on his left foot. "I never said shit to no one, man! Don't even try to accuse me of that shit! And never think I said anything to Double G. Him and me are finished." He dragged a finger across his throat. "That was a one-time thing. If I could do it over again, I wouldn't."

"Okay, Remo, okay. Relax."

"That's the truth, Cutler. I can't help whether you believe it or not." He was really getting upset. "I might have taken off with your money, but I never lied to you. Not once."

I stood. "You deal for Gillian."

"That's right."

"And you helped Double G because you thought he'd owe you one."

"That's for real." Remo spread his hands wide. "I thought maybe I was being smart—making plays for my future. I screwed up, and you made it right. What can I say?"

"You can start with you're sorry."

Remo closed his eyes. "Aw, shit, Cutler. You know I am."

"Or maybe I'll punch you in the teeth, and we'll call it even."

His eyes snapped open. "I'm sorry, man!" He clasped his hands together. "For real. I should never have done such a thing."

"Where'd you go in Mexico?"

"Cabo."

"And you met a girl?"

He smiled. "Oh, man, did I? She was so freakin' beautiful. You should have seen her, Cutler."

"Why'd you come back?"

"It got too hot."

"You got into some trouble?"

Embarrassment flashed through his eyes. "Her husband didn't take too kindly to what we were doing."

Even in Mexico, Remo's decision-making was questionable.

"This thing with Gillian—you only recommended me because you thought I could help?"

He nodded, and his hands went further apart. "That's the whole truth and nothing but."

I headed for the door. "Remo, do me a favor."

"What's that?"

"Don't recommend me to any more of your friends."

***

I walked up the street to my little house. A business card was slipped in between the screen door and the frame.

Inside the house, I tossed the card onto my desk. I opened my cell phone and noticed a text. It was from a number not in my phone.

MR. CUTLER—PLEASE CALL WHEN YOU HAVE A MOMENT. GILLIAN.

I put the phone on the desk and went into the backyard. A large German Shepherd ambled over from a shaded corner of the yard.

"Hey, buddy."

He wagged his tail.

"Time for some ball?"

The tail swished faster.

Corporal and I entered the house. I grabbed one of his now gray tennis balls on the way back through. We walked across the street to A.M. Cannon Park. The swimming pool and basketball courts were always active at this time of year. The large swaths of green grass were usually free of visitors, though.

I threw the ball, and the dog chased it.

When I first got Corporal, I made sure to run him through his exercises daily. He'd been raised by a former Marine and taught to respond to Drill and Ceremony commands. When his owner was murdered, I adopted the dog. I was worried that he might forget the commands and that some freak might take advantage of him someday.

As time passed, though, I became less worried about that. Instead, he became more of my pal—perhaps even my best friend. We played ball every day and went to many places together.

I'm not sure how old he was, but he was past four—I knew that much. The question of how long German Shepherds lived bothered me lately, but I was afraid to search out the answer.

We played in the heat for about twenty minutes. By then, the dog's tongue hung sideways from his mouth, and his gait was considerably slower.

Back at the house, Corporal lapped up an entire bowl of water. I refilled it, and he polished off half of that. Afterward, I let him into the backyard.

My cell phone rang.

It was a number I knew.

I answered it. "Hey."

"What are you doing tonight?"

I shrugged even though she couldn't see it. "Nothing."

"Just what I hoped you were doing," she said. "Wanna come over?"

***

It was shortly after ten when I arrived. The front door opened without my knocking, and Stacy Mathers appeared. She wore a white, terry cloth robe and a bright smile.

"You made it," she whispered.

"Of course I did. You called."

She grabbed my hand and pulled me in. "Be quiet. I got them to sleep early tonight."

Stacy had two kids. The boy was five, and the girl was four. I'd never met them. That was part of our deal.

For a time, I dated her sister, Tanya. That's not true. I *saw* Tanya—we never dated. Tanya would come to my place when I lived in the Claremont Apartments. I had no idea where she lived. I did know that Tanya was the ex-wife of one of the wealthiest men in town and that she'd been a runner-up for Miss Teen Washington. Tanya was clumsily making her way through the latter half of her thirties, and I was part of that ungracefulness.

Unfortunately, I might have been in love with Tanya.

Stacy disapproved of how her sister treated me like a disposable lover. She also might have disapproved of how Tanya treated the other men in her life. Stacy never told me any of that, though. I picked it up in the offhanded comments she made now and then. But I learned about Stacy's disappointment in her sister on the first night we met. Stacy was recently divorced and called to 'talk.' She said she wanted a man's perspective about why her marriage failed.

It was a strange request from a woman I'd never met, but I agreed. She sounded hurt and lost. I didn't worry about how she got my number—the landline is listed in the phonebook. We met at a bar halfway between both of our homes. One drink led to a second, which led to another, which led to a drunken tryst in my truck.

Since then, we'd become lovers just like her sister and I were. But now, the roles were reversed. Stacy never came to my place; I went to hers only after the kids were asleep.

We weren't disposable lovers. Instead, we were convenient.

I'm not sure if she saw other men, but I doubted it. I no longer had a girlfriend, but that didn't mean I was monogamous. It wasn't that kind of relationship, and we didn't discuss if it needed to be. I liked her well enough for it to be more than it was, but Stacy didn't want it that way.

She said it was because of the kids, and I chose to believe her.

Those were her rules, and I played within them.

Stacy closed the door behind me and locked it. She spun around, opened the terry cloth robe, and let it fall to the floor.

She didn't waste any time.

Chapter 4

I awoke in my own bed. I'd left Stacy's place shortly after two. She didn't want me mixing with the kids in the morning, and I understood why. I had my own daughter who was now fourteen and living in the Seattle area with her mother. Protecting Erin from my love life had never been much of a concern, but it probably should have been.

The last time Erin met a girlfriend of mine was a couple of years ago. Even though they only spent a short time together, Erin liked that one. When that relationship imploded, Erin blamed me, and why wouldn't she? I had a history of broken relationships starting with her mother. Maria and I never married, so Erin drew a line of failure from her mother throughout my entire love life.

I stopped talking to Erin about my girlfriends. Because of that, I had no problem with how Stacy treated our arrangement. If a woman ever entered my life who wanted to be something more than occasional, I would have a decision to make.

After a shower and a shave, I made breakfast—three hard eggs with burnt toast and a slathering of jam. The toast wasn't supposed to be burned, and the eggs were meant to be over easy. The jam was perfect since it was store-bought. I'm a lousy cook due to inattentiveness and the willingness to eat about anything.

When I finished breakfast, I checked my cell phone. There was another text message from Gillian—PLS CALL.

Instead, I texted her back. I'd gotten pretty good at communicating this way. When Erin wanted something, she sent text messages. I'd go days without hearing from her, and then there'd be a flurry of electronic banter. She hated calling, which I thought was odd, but I'd connect with my daughter in whatever ways she wanted.

I was still slow at pressing the number pad several times to bumble out a message, but I was getting better. My message to Gillian was simple—I'LL BE OUT BY 10.

Less than three seconds later, she responded—THX!

I puttered around the office, which was in my living room. There wasn't much for me to do that morning—I simply wanted to feel busy. No cases were active, and no invoices were outstanding, but my accounts were flush now—at least by my standards. Not only had my last client paid promptly, but Gillian covered Remo's debt which I had essentially written off.

Before heading out to East Trent, I stopped by the bank and deposited most of the cash. Having that much money in my pocket felt great, but who was I kidding? It would burn a hole in there sooner or later. Best to get it out so I wouldn't be tempted to do something stupid.

I drove east to see just what kind of setup Gillian Brewer had created.

***

The building was on Trent Avenue—the old state highway that provided quick east-west travel before Interstate-90 reduced its usefulness sometime in the sixties. Even so, there was still a fair amount of traffic for a Monday morning.

I located the property courtesy of Gillian's business card. I should have realized that the building wouldn't have been too hard to find, knowing that it had recently been broken into.

A large piece of plywood covered the window of Sunshine Smiles Tanning Salon.

The building had three small units. Each bay had a large glass window and an entrance door to its right. Above each unit was a box sign with painted plastic that I imagined would illuminate at night. To the far left—the east—was the tanning salon. In the middle bay was a screen-printing business—Dandy Designs. And at the west end was the nail salon—Naomi Nail.

I pulled into the lot and considered the last shop's sign. It was newer, as were the other signs. Not only was Naomi not in the possessive form, but it appeared she only worked on a single nail. Had the sign designer made a mistake, and Gillian hung the sign anyway? And who was Naomi? Gillian told me she owned the business.

As soon as I climbed out of my truck, a powerful chemical smell greeted me. It was sharp and offensive. I shook it away and wondered if it came from the screen-printing business. I'd never been inside a nail salon. Could they use chemicals that harsh?

A morning breeze swept across the small parking lot. Some scraps of paper fluttered by, and a used coffee cup flipped end over end. For a moment, I was thankful for the small gust as it cleared the chemical aroma, but it brought an odd scent with it—a putrid, cloying odor that turned my stomach. It reminded me of death—of rotten meat, perhaps. I turned and searched for it.

When the breeze stopped, death's bouquet vanished and was replaced by the chemical smell. Like sniffing a carton of spoiled milk for a second time, I carefully inhaled as if hoping to prove what I already knew. Death was out there somewhere, hiding under the sharp chemical fragrance.

I pinched my nose and stepped onto the sidewalk under the building's awning. That's when I noticed a security camera at the east end. There was a sister to it at the west end, too.

An electronic bell announced my entrance into Sunshine Smiles with a pleasant bing-bong. The Pussycat Doll's "Don't Cha" played softly in the background. I knew the song from my time working at Club Royale.

There was a small lobby with a couple of chairs and a coffee table filled with magazines like *People*, *Us*, and *Entertainment Weekly*. I'd recently seen a couple of them on the grocery store newsstand.

In the far corner sat a cinder block. It was likely the one that had come through the window. There was no other reason for it to be in the lobby.

Behind the receptionist's counter were a couple of short walls that led to a narrow hallway. On both sides of the hallway were a series of doors.

The business smelled of coconut oil and disinfectant. There was an odd hum as if a heavy fan was working somewhere. I concentrated for a moment and decided it was underneath me. If I hadn't known there was a basement grow, I wondered if I would have even suspected a fan might be there.

A security camera above the desk watched the lobby.

A door opened from the opposite end of the hallway and closed with a heavy thud. A moment later, a second door shut. Gillian soon appeared. She wore a white t-shirt, red shorts, and white sandals. A simple red bandana held her hair back. Her face broadened with what seemed to be a genuine smile.

"Thank you for coming."

I nodded.

"Remo said you two talked."

"I wanted to know a little more about your history with him."

Gillian wiped her hands with a rag. "So, what did you find? That we're associates with some history?"

"A lot of history, I'd say."

"He was the inspiration for me to get started in the business."

I pointed at the boarded-up window. "That's a big mess. How many days has it been?"

"Three."

"Why hasn't it been replaced yet?"

Gillian stood near the window. She knocked on the plywood with the back of her fist. "It's a big piece of glass, and the company I use was already booked on another job."

"Can't you call someone else?"

"I don't do business with strangers. My business requires a certain level of familiarity and a certain level of trust. I can't build that overnight."

Gillian's whole life was built around everyone doing their job and keeping what they saw to themselves. If she limited exposing the operation unnecessarily to others, maybe her circle of influence was small enough that she was right—there was a leak.

That's why she had to go through the rigmarole with Remo. Bringing his account current wasn't an act of generosity to placate me. It was meant to keep her circle of influence small. She couldn't go around interviewing private detectives, especially if one of them had a moral code stricter than mine. The cops could end up on her doorstep quicker than she could say silence is golden.

I looked out the glass door. There were no other vehicles besides mine. When I turned back to her, I motioned down the hall. "Is anyone using the equipment now?"

"Look around. It's okay."

I entered the hallway. Behind each door was a bulky tanning machine. The equipment appeared to be well-maintained, and the vinyl floors were clean.

"Looks like you've got a decent thing going here," I said.

Her smile was kind. "Not really but thank you."

"I know it's a cover, but—"

She held up a hand to interrupt me. "You're not understanding. Anybody who really cares about tanning isn't coming here."

I pointed at the nearest tanning machine. "That doesn't work?"

"It works. They all do. They must just in case the law shows up for whatever reason, be it a health inspector or the fire marshal. But those machines are all the same—they're low-pressure beds." Gillian entered the small room and rested a hand on the cumbersome machine. "Real salons want different beds, so their customers don't get tan lines from over usage." She motioned along the side of her body. "They'll have high-pressure beds so the UV rays can get deeper into the skin. They'll also have a booth—" she rolled her eyes "—I mean, a stand-up bed so customers can get an all-around tan." She raised her arms above her head. "Get it?"

I saw her point.

"Those salons will also focus on additional services like spray tans, or maybe they'll bring in an esthetician to draw in other customers."

"A what?"

"Someone who can provide skin care services like microblading and chemical peels."

"I'm at a loss."

She chuckled. "Let's just say they provide services that I won't. We have no interest in attracting more customers."

I leaned against the opened room's door jamb. "How many customers do you have?"

"Now, that's the question, isn't it?" Gillian stepped into the hallway. When she turned around, she dropped her shoulders onto the nearest wall and shoved her hands into her pockets. Her hips jutted out toward me. In another situation, I might have found it suggestive.

She continued. "A few gals from the neighborhood come in because it's convenient, but that's the only reason people come here. My prices aren't competitive, and I don't give discounts. Never once. Anyone willing to shop around knows they can get a better deal elsewhere."

"You don't want business?"

Gillian smirked. "Why would I? My client list is already full."

I cocked my head as I put the pieces together. "Your client list is bogus. All of this—" I motioned toward the hulking machine in the room behind me "—is for show."

"Can you prove that, Officer Cutler?"

Six rooms were attached to the hallway, each containing a rarely used tanning machine.

I snapped my fingers. "You're laundering your drug money through the business."

"That's part of it. Let's go next door."

She led me outside. When I exited, she stopped and locked the door.

"You're the only employee?" I asked.

"I've got a girl who works for me, but today is her day off. Dawn'll be in tomorrow morning if you want to check her out. Or I can give you her address if you want to interview her away from the business, whichever works best for you." Gillian strode over to Dandy Designs and pulled open the door.

When I stepped inside, the sharp chemical odor overwhelmed me. I winced and turned away. "Christ," I muttered.

Gillian held my arm by the elbow. "Hold on. We'll only be a minute."

A man wearing a gas mask stepped from the back room. He pulled it up over the top of his head. He was in his early forties with short, sandy brown hair. Even from this distance, I could see the highlights in it. "Hey, Gilly," he said.

She waved slightly. "Hi, Eddie." Her hand slid up to my shoulder. "Just showing my friend the building."

"Need me?"

"Nope." She shook her head.

Eddie put the rubber mask over his face and disappeared into the room.

"Let's go," Gillian said. "That's all I wanted to show you."

On the sidewalk, I breathed deeply to clear out the chemical stench, but it remained powerful outside.

"There's no escaping the smell," I said. "It's even out here."

"That's sort of the point."

I hadn't seen her grow yet, but I imagined it would be significant if it were in the basement of this building. She would need a way to disguise the odor of marijuana. Layering a chemical stink over top of it seemed a smart way to start.

Gillian tapped the window of the screen-printing shop. "We vent the odor over the roof and let it waft down here."

"And Eddie hangs out there all day with a gas mask on?"

She nodded. "We change the filters often. He sits there with cans of chemicals opened and the fans running. It's an OSHA violation, but no one has complained."

"Does he know how to print?"

"Sure. He occasionally does something for himself when he gets bored."

"Just in case the law pokes its nose inside?"

"Or some curious customer. But they'll never get to submit an order. We're always overbooked and weeks behind."

"Your client list," I said.

"Exactly."

I put my hands on my hips. "You've got money laundering and the marijuana smell covered."

The morning breeze returned and cleared out the chemical aroma. The brief reprieve brought along with it the stench of death.

"But what is *that* smell?" I asked.

"The rendering plant." Gillian crinkled her nose. "It's where they process dead animals and do other things I don't want to know about. It's over there." She pointed in a circular fashion that made me believe it was somewhere behind her building.

"Is the smell always like that?"

"Not always, but in the summer, it gets pretty rancid. Can you imagine working there?"

I shook my head.

"I can handle the chemical smell a lot better than that. Probably because it doesn't coincide with me imagining a building filled with dead horses." She touched my arm. "Let's step into Naomi's."

A brass bell tinkled as we entered the nail salon. The suite was brightly lit, and small white tables filled most of the space. A glass receptionist counter was near the front. Some soft zither music played throughout the area.

Only two women were in the business—both were Asian and in their early forties. They sat on opposite sides of a table near the back. One woman held her hand out as if she were getting her nails done. The other leaned over the first woman's hand studiously—a nailbrush was clutched in her fingers.

The woman with the nailbrush didn't look up when she said in a heavy accent, "Come back tomorrow. All book up."

Gillian said, "Good morning, Hue."

The woman lifted her head and leaned back upon hearing Gillian's voice.

The other woman pulled her hand back and turned in her chair.

"Still getting the same nails done, Thi?" Gillian asked.

Thi turned her hand to reveal that only three fingernails were done on her left hand.

Gillian leaned toward me. "Thi's never gotten all of her nails done."

"She's here every day?"

"There's another gal that switches off now and then, but Hue is here most days."

"So, who's Naomi?"

Gillian eyed me. "You don't know anything about the nail business."

I shook my head. "Can we step outside? This place is giving me a headache."

The business stunk of chemicals, and I couldn't determine if it was the screen-printing joint or coming from inside the nail business.

"Bye, ladies," Gillian said.

They watched us with suspicion as we turned to leave.

The chemical smell was slightly less outside, but it was still pungent. I pinched my nose and followed Gillian back into Sunshine Smiles. There was only the smell of coconut oil in there.

"How do you stand the chemicals?" I asked.

"You get used to it." She stepped behind the counter. "Would you know there was a grow here if I hadn't told you?"

I shook my head but latched onto something from my law enforcement days. "There would be a heat signature coming from this building. If anyone at the power company were looking for strange amounts of power being used in conjunction with grow lights…"

As my words trailed off, a smile appeared on Gillian's face.

"Son of a bitch," I said and pointed to the floor. "You don't have the tanning salon to launder money. It's to hide your power usage."

"All three businesses launder my money," Gillian said. "The building, too. I pay rent to myself, but the tanning salon is specifically to hide the electricity that the grow lights use."

"But what about at night when the salon is closed? Won't the power company see the power usage all day?"

Gillian's brow furrowed. "The plants work on the same circadian rhythm we do—night and day, day and night. If we always gave them light, it would freak them out. When we go to sleep, the plants go to bed."

"I wouldn't take you as the type to smoke weed."

She lightly snickered. "You think there's a type? That's the cop in you showing, John. Everybody smokes. From high school kids up to the president."

"The president doesn't smoke."

"The former president did."

"But he didn't inhale."

Gillian smirked. "Uh-huh. I believe *that*. Mark my words. Someday it's going to be legal."

"I highly doubt that, but what will you do if it does?"

"Are you kidding? I'll embrace it and happily move to the legitimate side. I will have had all this experience with growing, distribution, and sales. I'll be light years ahead of my competition. I'll run them over like a bulldozer." She smacked her hands together and pushed one out in front of the other like a rocket ship headed toward the moon.

I studied her. She intimidated me when we first met because she owned three businesses and a commercial building. Now, I was only slightly impressed and not the least bit intimidated. She was a criminal who had learned how to game the system. I had to give her credit for doing so, though. She'd figured it out better than anyone I'd met during my time on the street.

"So," I said, "do you want to show me why I'm really here?"

"I thought you'd never ask."

***

At the end of the hallway was a door. It looked like any other, except the lock was busted.

"This is the vandals' handiwork," Gillian said.

She pulled the door open, and we faced another—this one was steel. The exterior of the building was concrete block. I'm unsure what the interior was framed with, but I imagined it to be wood. The door would certainly slow someone down, but if an intruder was bound and determined to get in—they would. Perhaps Gillian had the interior wall reinforced somehow.

The steel door's lock was a numbered keypad.

"Who installed the door for you?"

"A contractor. One with a good reputation."

"Did they know what you planned to do with the basement?"

"I told them I wanted to build a safe room. I gave them a story about an abusive ex-husband."

I eyed her. "Remo said you were married before. Maybe your ex-husband is involved with the break-in."

"We weren't divorced, and if he were involved in this, I'd be impressed. He died in a motorcycle accident about ten years ago."

She didn't seem broken up by his death. Maybe time had healed that wound.

"A zombie ex trying to steal my grow would make for a whole set of different problems. I'd probably call *Ghostbusters* before you."

Gillian entered a code into the keypad—she made sure I didn't see it. A lock clicked back, and she pushed the door open.

A hulking white man with a shotgun stood at the bottom of the stairs.

I spun out of the way and tried to pull Gillian with me.

"Hey, Rock," Gillian said. "Everything's cool."

"You sure?" the man at the bottom of the stairwell asked.

"I'm with John Cutler, a friend of mine. We're coming down."

"Yeah, okay, Gilly."

I asked, "Who the hell is that?"

"I've had to hire some extra security." She motioned into the basement. "Watch your step—the first one is a doozy."

"By all means, you first."

"I need to close the doors. Don't be scared of Rock. He won't shoot you. Not now, at least."

I peeked around the corner to ensure the big man had moved away from the bottom of the stairs. Usually, I wouldn't enter a stairwell knowing that an armed man waited for me. The fatal funnel was so named for that reason.

The initial stair was double the height of a standard step. The security door was set back from the first, which required the floor to be extended into the stairwell. Even to my untrained eye, the set-up violated various safety laws.

I looked back at Gillian. "You mentioned a fire inspector earlier. What happens if one of them shows up? Or a safety regulator?"

"Why would they come? They only come when a business first opens or if someone complains. And no one is complaining from my team." Gillian called into the basement, "Are you going to complain, Rock?"

"Not me. No way."

She smiled. "There you go."

We clomped down the stairs. Rock had moved into a nearby corner. He cradled the shotgun in the crook of his arm. He had shoulder-length black hair and a five o'clock shadow even though it was still morning. He wore a black t-shirt, dirty blue jeans, and heavy black boots. A Colt 1911 was holstered to his hip.

Gillian said to the security man, "Would you mind waiting for us upstairs?"

Rock nodded. "Sure thing."

"Thanks, and I'll keep an eye on the camera in case a real customer shows up for a tan."

When the big man was gone, I surveyed the basement. It was as large as the entire building. The outer walls and ceiling were lined with shiny fabric.

"Foylon," Gillian explained.

Ducting ran around the ceiling, and an A/C unit hummed quietly.

Near the stairs was a desk with a computer. Its monitor showed all the camera feeds from the building—there were nine. Shown were the parking lot, the interior of the three businesses, and the back of the building.

The room was comfortable even though it felt humid due to the number of marijuana plants lined up in rows. The skunky aroma from the plants was cloying.

"How many plants do you have?" I asked.

"A hundred. I could fit more in, but that would jam them together and affect the quality. They need to have room and access to the light. Besides, I like the round number. Makes it easier for me to do the math."

Fluorescent lights hung throughout the basement.

I stepped forward and inspected the first plant. The leaves were wide and a deep olive-green color.

Gillian moved next to me. "This is an Indica strain." She waved her hand in the direction of the whole crop. "That's what I'm growing here. It's recommended to give each plant two to four feet to grow. I went on the high side."

"No pun intended."

"Funny." She didn't sound like she thought it was.

"How big is the building?"

"Forty-five hundred square feet. Basement is the same size, but I lose space to the stairwell. Plus, I need supplies down here, so take away at least five hundred for that."

"Huh." I stepped deeper into the basement forest and let the leaves play across my arms. "How much product can you get from one of these plants?"

Gillian followed me and inspected another of the flowers. "That's a tough question since every plant is different, and indoor plants are about half the production of outdoor plants. I wish I could grow this outdoors, but this is our lot in life."

"So, how much?"

She wiggled the leaf she now held. "On average, one of these plants will give about a quarter pound of bud. Give or take. I'm taking a little more than that with what I've got going here."

"That still doesn't sound like much."

"A quarter pound is equal to four ounces."

"I know the math."

"Every ounce is four hundred bucks."

My eyebrows shot up. "That's $1,600 per plant." I stood on my tiptoes. "A hundred plants." I dropped back to my heels. "That's $160,000 of weed."

"About, and that's before it's rolled up and sold as joints. Every quarter pound makes roughly two-hundred twenty-five."

"If a joint is five bucks—"

"Which would be a helluva deal to a high school kid."

I let the comment hang in the air. Did I want my daughter to smoke weed when she got to high school? I'd tried it a couple of times at that age but never took to it. I preferred drinking far more. I didn't want Erin doing either. I decided I didn't want to go down the morality road any further. It would remind me of all my wrong choices and would only make me sound like a hypocrite.

"That skunky smell," I said. "It's thick down here. How do you stop it from going out?"

"I can't stop all of it, but I try. The whole room is sealed. Almost no air gets out that we don't want except when we walk through the door upstairs. That's my only weak point, and I need to be careful of it." She pointed to two contraptions on opposite walls. Both were attached to air-ducting. "Those are scrubbers. They use carbon filters to remove the smell before the air goes outside. There's another scrubber outside that's pumping in clean air."

"To remove the screen-printing chemicals and the rendering funk."

"That's right. I'm not sure if those aromas would do anything to the plants, but I don't want to find out."

"How long does it take them to grow?"

"Until maturity, it's about six to eight months, then we harvest and start over."

"You're clearing $160,000 every eight months?"

"I wish." Gillian shook her head. "I just got the operation this big. And don't forget there are expenses. I've got utilities and a mortgage. I pay Hue and Eddie through my company. Everyone else gets paid under the table, but that's still gotta come out of the pot."

"Another pun."

She smirked. "It was unintentional, I assure you. My point is that I do well, but not as well as you're thinking."

"You're not paying taxes."

"I pay taxes."

I cocked my head.

"I pay property taxes on the building and sales taxes for the businesses."

"But you're not paying taxes related to the sales of the marijuana itself."

"Well, no. Of course not."

I walked over to the computer. On the screen were various video feeds. Three exterior cameras showed a bright sunny day. Two were for the front, and one was obviously on the back.

My truck was parked in the front, and its license plate was easily readable on one camera feed.

There was a white Audi A4 and a motorcycle that I guessed to be a Harley in the backlot. Something was painted on the bike's gas tank, but I couldn't get a good look at it from the camera's angle. Neither vehicle's plates could be read.

I couldn't imagine Rock driving the Audi, but how had the shotgun arrived if he rode the motorcycle? He wouldn't have been so brazen as to carry that on his back, would he? And he wouldn't have brought it in a side pouch like in some *Mad Max* movie.

Maybe the shotgun was always here. Gillian had an illegal grow protected by various levels of subterfuge and security. Owning a shotgun didn't seem so far out of the realm of possibilities.

I asked, "Where'd you find Rock?"

"He's my brother-in-law."

Or maybe Gillian had brought the shotgun in her car. Did it even matter how it got there? I decide to drop it.

The other feeds showed the interior of the stores and the basement.

Rock stood at the counter reading a magazine in the tanning salon above us. I couldn't see the shotgun. Was it under the counter? Why was I so worried about it? Maybe because he'd recently pointed it at me. My gaze flitted to the other feeds.

Eddie wore his gas mask and walked around Dandy Designs. It looked like he was about to make something. At Naomi Nail, Hue and Thi sat at their table and laughed. There were only single feeds in the printing and nail salons, but the tanning salon had multiple camera angles.

There were two feeds in the basement. Gillian and I stood watching ourselves on the computer on one of them. There would be no denying to the cops that I was ever here.

"How long do you keep the footage?" I asked.

"Worried about being on *Candid Camera*?"

The look on my face probably gave it away.

"I don't want any more history than need be," she said. "Unless I save it, all footage is deleted after twenty-four hours. You can breathe easier now."

"I didn't realize I was holding my breath."

She smiled. "Do you want to see the footage of the break-in?"

Gillian leaned over the computer and clicked a button. A small window appeared, and she clicked on something else. Suddenly, all the camera feeds changed. Gone were Rock, Eddie, and the two women. The external feeds had morphed to night. The timestamp showed it be a bit after three in the morning.

An early '90s Ford pickup pulled into the parking lot. Its license plate was missing. Three men got out wearing ski masks. One of them reached into the truck bed and removed a cinder block. The two others grabbed crowbars. The guy with the block walked confidently over to the tanning salon's window and hucked it in. The glass shattered and rained down. The other men dragged the crowbars along the edge of the windowsill to remove any remaining shards.

"Do you have any sound?" I asked.

"No, but you have to imagine that made an amazing racket."

I considered Trent Avenue at three in the morning. The building sat immediately on the old highway. There wasn't much traffic at that time of the day. The speed was 35 MPH, and there were four lanes. Anyone driving by would need to look over at the right time to see something.

The extra time to use the crowbars along the windowsill should have felt like overkill to the guys involved. However, it seemed to be a wise precaution. Not only would it lessen the chance of getting cut on a random sliver of glass when stepping through the window, but it was one less thing for a passerby to notice and call the cops.

The man who threw the cinder block returned to the truck and reached into the bed. He returned with a massive pair of loppers.

When the three men entered the building, the two with the crowbars led the way toward the back. Gillian clicked one of the camera feeds to make it full screen.

One of the men jammed a crowbar into the first door and levered it. The second stepped next to him and did the same. For several moments, they heaved back and forth. The third man pulled on the knob until the door popped open.

The three seemed to cheer briefly. The jubilation immediately stopped. One man stepped forward and swung his crowbar overhead. I couldn't see or hear it hit the steel door—the limitations of the security camera forbade that.

There seemed to be some excited talk among the three men. The two with the crowbars set to work on levering the door. They quickly got frustrated and kicked at the door.

The first man—the one holding the loppers—checked his watch and then said something. He walked toward the front of the store. The other two quickly followed.

Gillian returned the window to its standard size, and the screen was again filled with the various camera feeds.

The three men climbed through the front window and returned to the white Ford pickup. It backed away and left the parking lot. Its back license plate was also missing.

Gillian paused the recorded feed. "What do you think? Want to see it again?"

"The loppers," I said. "Were they going to cut the plants and haul them out?"

"That's my guess."

"Are they ready to harvest?"

"Not yet."

"If they cut them down early, does that ruin their potency?"

Gillian nodded. "It does, but you can still smoke it."

"What if they were barely grown?"

She shrugged. "That's a good question. It's not like I need to follow the seasons to grow down here. This is essentially a greenhouse." Gillian pointed at the grow lights. "All things considered. Maybe they figured I'm following the season planting schedule, which I could harvest anywhere from now through October."

I stared at the paused video feeds. "That's a lot of trouble for a group of dopers. Are you butting heads with any other suppliers?"

"I don't think so. I've been doing this for a while, not at this location, mind you, but I'm not new to the game."

"How long have you been here?"

"Two and a half years. This is my third grow."

"Maybe it's a rival dealer. Occasionally, people get delusions of grandeur."

Her brow furrowed. "I don't know. I don't think so."

"No one comes to mind?"

Gillian shook her head.

"Who do you sell to?"

"I've got a few buyers. Middlemen, so to speak." She waggled her hand. "That's the gender-neutral men, you understand."

"Not just one?"

She shook her head. "I didn't want to be tied to a single person, single group. I figured doing so might give that other entity too much power."

"These middlemen. Do you trust them?"

"I do. And why would they bust in here and harvest early? I pointed it out earlier—they all knew about the security door." She tapped the monitor. "Those guys didn't."

"But Remo," I said. "You deal directly with him. Why not make him go through a middleman?"

"Consider that a favor since we go so far back. I've got a soft spot for him, but everyone else goes through intermediaries. Less hassle for me."

"You've been here for more than two years," I said, "but Remo's only been working for you about a year. What's up with that?"

"I lost track of him." She inhaled deeply and turned toward the small forest. "Cooper, that's my husband. He and I started to grow plants in our basement. We got a wild hair, sort of like those homebrewers do. The first one we grew was fun, and it felt like this weird accomplishment. After that, we no longer needed to buy from Remo. The next time, Cooper and I got a few plants going. Nothing crazy. When they matured, we sold most of them to our friends. You know, more as a goof than anything. We didn't need the money. Cooper had a good job. Mine not so much. Growing was something that made us feel like kids. Gave us that rush of fumbling in the backseat. There's not much of that once you get past twenty. When he died, I kept growing and selling. He was gone. The rush was gone. But there were still bills to pay."

"You expanded your operation?"

She nodded. "Out of my home to a farmhouse in the country. Made some connections along the way. Paid the bills that needed to be paid. Reinvested what I could. Expanded a little more."

"The American dream."

"Sans husband." Sadness crossed her face.

I didn't want to stay in the past, so I pointed at the paused video. "And you have no idea who these guys are."

"None."

"But you think they're coming back."

"Wouldn't you?"

I crossed my arms and studied the still picture. "If it were me, now that I know there's a steel door, I'd come back with an acetylene torch. Hell, maybe I'd just bust a hole in the back wall right above the stairs—that's probably the easiest thing to do."

"But there will be someone here at night from now on—either Rock or someone like him."

"Someone like him? You're letting more people in on your secret."

She waved a hand. "It can't be helped. What else am I supposed to do? I'm under attack."

"You'd best figure out a contingency plan. Like where can you move this stuff and start over."

Her face hardened. "I'm not starting over. I'm making this work. I put all my money into this building and these businesses. I'm finally at a point where I can start making a serious profit."

"But if you get exposed, and the cops find out—"

"That's why I need your help. Find the leak. Where did this attack come from?"

I glanced around the basement. Did I want to get involved with illegal drugs? No. But the problem seemed challenging enough that I wanted to poke around a little to see what I could find.

"Well?" she asked.

"You said double the fee."

"That's right. When can you get started?"

"Right now. I want the names of your employees and where they live."

Gillian moved toward the steps. "No problem, but I'm telling you, none of them are involved."

"Let me do this my way."

"Fine," she said. "You're the expert."

Chapter 5

Gillian and I returned upstairs. I waited as she closed the doors to the basement.

Rock stood near the front glass door like a sentry on watch. I still didn't see the shotgun. It must have been nearby. The gun on his hip would be more than enough.

When Gillian turned to me, I motioned toward the big man. "What about him?" I whispered.

She shook her head. "He's trustworthy."

"He's an employee."

"I already told you, he's my brother-in-law. That means something to us. Besides, he's known what I've been doing the whole time. It doesn't make any sense."

Rock looked in our direction. I lifted my chin to acknowledge him. He returned the gesture and then shifted his attention toward the front parking lot.

A heavy safety bar secured the rear door.

"Can we step out back?" I asked.

Gillian bent at the knees and heaved the steel bar upward and out of its two support arms. I caught the metal bar and rested it against the back wall.

Once outside, we shut the door behind us. The chemical smell caught me off-guard.

"Damn," I muttered.

"You get used to it," Gillian said.

Next to the building was a small gravel parking lot. Beyond that was a large dirt area littered with potholes and ruts. I imagined them filling up with water during a rainstorm.

Parked near the back door were the white Audi A4 and the motorcycle. I stepped over to it. On the gas tank was a custom-painted skull shrouded in smoke.

I pointed at the building. "Rock is a Wasted Soul?"

"Is that a problem?"

"For you."

She opened her hands. "It's not a problem. He's been with them since I've known him."

"Your husband," I said. "He died in a motorcycle accident. Was he with the Souls?"

Gillian shook her head. "No, Cooper and Hudson learned to ride from their dad. Rock took to the heavy bikes like this." She patted the Harley's gas tank. "My husband went for the fast ones—the crotch rockets, he called them. And Cooper was never into that club life. Let me assure you."

I cocked my head. "His nickname is Rock as in Rock Hudson?"

"The club gave it to him, and he wears it like a badge of honor. And Rock sounds tougher than the nickname his mother gave him as a boy—Huddie."

"All right then. Do the Souls know about your grow?"

"Rock has known since day one. I don't think he's ever told anyone. He kept our secrets, and we kept his. But I asked Rock for his help on this. He said he'd have to tell the club. I told him it was okay. What's wrong?"

"You've made your problem worse."

She moved around the bike to stand in front of me. "You think I can't trust my brother-in-law?"

"The Souls aren't known for their generosity."

"I know this is going to cost me. People don't work for free, especially when they find out how much money I'm making. Some even charge double."

I lifted my hands in mock surrender. "You offered. I didn't seek you out."

Gillian reached out but stopped short of touching my arm. "I'm sorry. It's just that I'm doing the best I can. Rock is family, and I trust that he's got my best interests at heart."

Bringing the Wasted Souls into the situation wasn't my problem. It was hers. I could always walk and return to my regularly scheduled life if it became an issue. She was stuck, though. Let Rock help her.

I looked away.

Beyond the gravel parking lot was a mobile home park. Several metal trailers were lined around a circular road. Interspersed among the rectangular homes were unhealthy-looking trees. A good windstorm might tip them over.

I motioned toward the trailer park. "Ever have problems with the renters?"

Gillian shook her head. "Why would I?"

"For starters, the smells from your businesses."

"By the time it gets to them, it's mixed in with everything else from this neighborhood." Gillian spread her arms, leaned her head back, and inhaled deeply. She looked like a circus showman about to start the main event. "You know what that smells like?"

"Carcinogens?"

She frowned. "Commerce. That's the smell of industry—the smell of money."

I eyed the mobile home park again. "They buy your product?"

"How would I know? I'm a grower. I never see the end-user. Only the buyers."

"The middlemen," I said. "And Remo."

"That's right, and all of them want me to succeed. My success is their success. I don't screw them on the price. You can forget it. None of them is the leak."

"I want their names, too."

Gillian's lips pursed. "I don't want to piss them off."

"You want to find out who did this or not?"

"I'll tell you what. Investigate everyone else first. If you strike out and need to start in on my network, then I'll give you all the names. Until then, I'd like to keep them confidential. Fair?"

"You don't know these people."

She cocked her head.

"Take Remo."

She shook her head in disbelief. "When will you cut that guy a break? He screwed up. Let it go."

"Remo told you he got in trouble for a job but did he tell you what he did?"

Gillian walked over to the Audi and leaned her butt against its front. "He did. He said he was a lookout on the heist of some payday loan operation."

Heist, I thought. That's the same word Remo used when he described it to me back in the spring. I thought it was funny then because people didn't use that word in polite conversation, and now here we were using it in a moderately civil discussion.

"Did he tell you who put the job together?"

"Some guy named Double G. What of it?"

I crossed my arms. So Remo had told her his name. "Have you ever heard of him before?"

"Not before Remo told me."

"What about Gary Gaspar? Ever heard of him?"

"Doesn't ring a bell."

"That's the same guy," I said. "Double G."

"Is there a point to this?"

"He's a scary guy who puts together heists."

She frowned. "No. Remo didn't say anything to him. I promise."

"It's one degree of separation from Double G to you. That makes me worried. It doesn't bother you?"

"It's Spokane, John. It's two degrees of separation for anyone. Hell, the first question out of most people's mouths in this town is, 'What high school did you go to?' Not what college. Folks around here wouldn't give a damn if you went to Harvard or Stanford. They want to know you went to schools with names like Gonzaga Prep or Shadle Park. And since you didn't grow up around here, that's a strike against you."

I held up a single finger. "Right now, Double G is in the shadows—one degree of separation from you." I pointed at the building. "Inside is a member of the Wasted Souls—"

"My brother-in-law."

"—an outlaw motorcycle gang—"

"That's taking it too far."

"—who now know for certain that you have a major grow in the basement."

"I figured it was better to pay the devil I know to stop the devil I don't."

"You say that until the moment they double-cross you."

She pushed off the car. "They aren't going to do that."

"Listen. I'm saying this—you need to be more careful than you are. You've got a nice set-up, but there are dangerous men about."

"And little ol' me can't take care of herself." She held her hands under her chin and batted her eyelids.

"You understand my point."

Her face darkened. "I can take care of myself."

"Then you don't need me."

I started for the corner of the building. Gillian trotted up beside me. She grabbed my arm to stop me.

"That's not what I meant," she said.

"I'm trying to point out that there are more threats than you realize. All of this might have been fun and games to start with, but you're on the razor's edge right now, and some bad shit could be headed your way."

She leaned forward. "Then help me avoid it."

"Close down the business and get out of the game. Hell, you can rent these spaces to legitimate businesses."

Gillian stepped back. "I'm not going to do that."

I turned and started walking again.

She hurried alongside me. "Where are you going?"

"To talk with Eddie."

"You're still working this thing?"

"Until I'm not. I need the info on your other employees."

She stopped walking. I didn't bother to look back.

***

Eddie Bersdorf and I stood behind the Dandy Designs suite. He'd left his gas mask inside the space then explained to me why he did it. He said, "I'm smarter than I look," which probably didn't take much.

His left eye turned slightly inward, which gave him a cross-eyed appearance. An old scar across his lower lip made it look permanently fat. He'd busted his nose somewhere in his life, and the bridge was forever swollen.

Eddie looked to be in his forties. Maybe he had a rough childhood. Or perhaps he'd just had a single accident that dealt him all that facial damage. Whatever caused it wasn't the reason I was there.

He shook a cigarette loose from a pack of Marlboros and slipped it between his lips. He extended the pack toward me, but I shook my head.

"You cool with me smoking?"

"Sure."

He flipped open a Zippo, dragged the roller over his jeans to spark it, then lit the cigarette. He pulled deeply on it, held the smoke as if he were hitting a joint, then exhaled. "You seem all right for a cop."

"I'm not a cop."

Eddie cocked his head. "Gillian said you were a detective."

"Private."

He pointed the two fingers that held the cigarette. "Right. Right. Like Philip Marlowe and Sam Spade. You ever read them?"

I nodded. "Marlowe."

"I read a lot in there. Kind of a pain with the mask on, but you get used to it." He inhaled on the cigarette again. "So, you're what? Working to find out who broke into the tanning salon?"

"That's right."

"You don't think it's some random dumb asses?"

"Is that what you think?"

"Who knows what to think?" Eddie motioned toward Rock's motorcycle. "Things just got interesting, didn't they?"

"Does that bother you?"

He shrugged. "I'm fine with it." He didn't sound like it. "I'm just saying things got interesting, you know."

I pulled the notebook from my pocket. "Where do you live?"

"Why?"

"Because I'm asking."

He inhaled on the cigarette and held it for a moment. "An apartment up in Hillyard." It was a poorer neighborhood in north Spokane. I wouldn't have expected a guy who wore a gas mask all day to live in Liberty Lake.

"What's the address?"

"You really need that?"

"Are you hiding something?"

"No." He rattled off an address. "I just don't like strangers knowing where I live."

"How long have you known Gillian?"

Eddie started to take another hit off the cigarette but paused. "Oh, geez. I don't know." He made a couple of small circular motions with his hand. "Maybe twenty years, I guess."

"How'd you guys meet?"

"Through a friend."

"Which friend?"

"Guy named Remo. You probably don't know him."

"I know Remo."

Eddie smiled. "Guy gets around, doesn't he? But he's a good dude. Salt of the earth type, as they say. We go all the way back to high school. We went to Rogers. Where'd you go?"

"Not from around here."

He seemed disappointed in that. It was just like Gillian had said, and it wasn't my first time experiencing it. There was an unwritten code—a secret handshake if you will—that attending high school in the Spokane area made you a local. Anyone who wasn't a Highlander, a Panther, or any other local mascot was deemed a latecomer and regarded with open suspicion.

"I ran around with Remo when we were in school. That's how I met Gilly back in the day. You think she's pretty now. Wow. You should have seen her back then." He blew on his knuckles and then waved them as if putting out a fire. "Freakin' heartbreaker."

"Who've you told about Gillian's operation?"

Eddie studied the end of his cigarette. "I've been thinking about that. You know, like, had I let something slip? But I can honestly say I haven't told nobody."

"No friends? No family?"

He eyed me. "Ah man, fuck that noise. Like I'd tell my friends what I'm doing. They'd all want me to score them free chronic. I work for my bud. They should work for theirs, too. As far as they know, I'm busting my hump in a lousy print shop."

"And your family?"

"They think I'm unemployed." He waved around his cigarette. "I'm not close with my parents, and I'm okay with it that way."

"Who were you worried that you might have told?"

He shrugged. "Some chick, maybe." Eddie flicked the end of his cigarette and knocked off some ash. "I'm not exactly Tom Cruise, so I gotta lay it on a little thick at times."

"And you've told them about working at a grow?"

"Hell no." His brow furrowed. "But I always have weed, and that's gotten me some trim that I probably shouldn't have gotten. Maybe they put two and two together." Eddie shook his head. "That doesn't seem right, though. They probably think I just got a good hook-up."

A breeze blew through and pushed away the chemical stink. It brought along the smell of the rendering plant.

Eddie's face pinched. "Phew, it's bad today."

"That bothers you, but the chemicals don't?"

He popped the cigarette back into his mouth and inhaled. "Safer to smoke out here than breathe in that shit."

I didn't want to correct his argument, so I asked, "Why do you think the attack on the salon was random?"

"Hell, I don't know." Eddie waved his cigarette again. "Can things just be bad luck? That's what I told Gilly. It comes for everybody at some time." He pointed at his face. "How do you think I ended up like this? I wasn't born this way."

"But they came prepared," I said. "They had a cinder block and crowbars."

"Sure, they came prepared, but that's how those smash and grab types are. They're probably the same sons a' bitches who bust into convenience stores to steal ATMs."

"But a tanning salon?"

He kicked some pebbles away. "Those beds gotta be worth a few grand, right? Maybe more?"

"They didn't go after even one, and do you think a couple of guys could drag one out and throw it in the bed of a truck?"

Eddie frowned. "Hell if I know, man. It's just a theory. I don't break the law." He sucked on his cigarette a final time, then flicked it to the back of the gravel lot. "I'm a working man. Ask a criminal if you want to know why they picked this place. You know, like they did with that Hannibal Lecter guy in that one movie."

***

When I went into Naomi Nail, only Hue remained. She looked up from a magazine as I entered the store. The chemical smell was sharp, but I did my best to ignore it. I had a job to do and could get through it quickly.

"Where's Thi?" I asked.

"She went to get us some lunch. She'll be back soon."

I cocked my head.

"What?"

"What happened to the broken English?"

She smiled. "That was for show, but if it makes you feel better..." Her smile melted. "Gillian say you a number one okay. Wanna do nail?" She pronounced Gillian's name with a guttural G. "Is that better?"

"I can do without it. Thanks."

Hue motioned toward a chair. "Take a load off." The cadence of her speech was off from someone who grew up in the country, but the words she'd spoken so far were perfect.

The chemicals inside the salon were worse than I expected. I pinched my nose. "Can we step out back?"

"Not so tough, are you?"

I moved toward the back door.

Hue stood. "It does not bother me anymore. It took some time, but I got used to it." She thumped her chest with her fist. "That is why we are the more hardy of the species."

"The Vietnamese?"

Her eyes narrowed. "Women."

I led her through the back door. It didn't have the same amount of security as Sunshine Smiles. It had a simple deadbolt and a knob lock.

Outback, the chemical smell was still there but less intense than inside Naomi Nail. We were basically in the same spot I stood with Eddie just a few minutes earlier, except maybe twenty feet further east.

I took some time to study her. Hue was short, a few inches over five feet, and in her early forties. Her skin was the color of overly creamed coffee. I wondered if she might have had an Anglo father. She wore a light blue shirt, dark blue pants, and sandals. Her toenails were painted pink, but her fingernails were clear.

I pulled out my notebook. "Hue, what's your last name?"

"Pham. Pham Hue."

She didn't have to clarify the Vietnamese naming convention, but she likely had to do it plenty of times before. I'd learned it while working as an officer in Seattle. "Where do you live?"

Her eyes narrowed. "Why do you need that?"

"Gillian explained what I was investigating?"

"Yes." Hue waggled a finger like a scolding teacher. "But I was not part of what happened. You do not need to see my home."

"What don't you want me to see?"

"Nothing." She seemed defensive now. "Gillian has been to my home. She can come." Her brow furrowed. "But not you. You no come." Her anger caused her to slip into broken English.

I lowered the notepad. "Did I do something to upset you?"

"You the police." Hue's face pinched, and she looked away. She inhaled deeply before facing me again. "You *are* the police."

It's the same thing Eddie had accused me of. I briefly wondered if they talked together.

"I'm a private investigator."

"But you work with the police. You share what you learn." She tapped the fingers of one hand into the open palm of another. "I know."

"I don't do that."

Hue eyed me with distrust.

"I promise."

"Your promise does not mean anything." She pointed at the Naomi Nail space, and then she motioned to my notebook. "I work there. Write that down. I will give you my phone number." She recited the digits. "You can call me if you need, but you will not come to my home."

There was no need for me to continue the struggle for her address. Gillian would tell me where all her employees lived.

"How long have you known Gillian?" I asked.

"A long time." It was a defiant answer.

I wasn't sure why things had turned hostile between us.

"How'd you meet?"

"At the college," she said.

"We're you in the same class?"

Hue shook her head. "I never went to university."

"But you said—"

She rolled her eyes. "We worked in the cafeteria. She was part-time to help pay for her education, and I was full-time to pay the rent."

"What college was this?"

"Does that matter?"

I turned my palms upward in an I-don't-know gesture.

She blinked several times, then pointed west. "The community college."

"You became friends while working in the cafeteria?"

Hue pursed her lips. "She was writing a report on Vietnam, so I introduced her to my mother who shared her story." Hue's face softened at the mention of her mother. "I translated for them. Gillian was very nice, very respectful. My mother had a hard time during the war. She had to do many bad things to survive—things a young woman should not have to do. She did not like telling me those things, but she wanted me to know. It helped to have Gillian there. It gave her an excuse to talk."

Hue stared down at her sandals and wriggled her toes.

She continued. "Gillian listened to everything my mother said and wrote it down. She talked for hours. So long, I learned many things that day. Gillian wrote a very good report. I still have a copy and read it when I miss my mother. She died many years ago."

Hue wriggled her toes some more.

"Gillian got an incomplete." Hue looked up and shrugged. "My mother's story was not the assignment she was supposed to do. She was to write about the Vietnam economy and its imports and exports. It was not supposed to be about history and politics. The professor liked the report, so he did not fail her. She had to redo the assignment. My mother did not help the second time."

"You stayed friends all these years?"

Hue nodded. "Gillian is a respectable woman. It is good to know people like that in your life. I hope she thinks of me as the same." She lowered her head and muttered, "Kiernan."

"Excuse me?"

"I live on Kiernan Avenue." She looked up and rattled off the numbers. "I am sorry that I did not tell you sooner. If you need to visit my home to prove to Gillian that I did not do this, then please come. I will give you my house keys if you want. I have nothing to hide."

"I don't think that will be necessary."

She studied her toes.

"Have you told anybody about what you do?"

Hue shook her head.

"Not even your husband?"

"I do not have a husband. I have no family." Her gaze challenged me. "I know better than to talk to anybody about my business. My mother taught her lessons well."

I closed my notebook and slid it into my pocket.

"Thank you for your time, Hue."

Chapter 6

If I wanted to continue working on Gillian's problem, there were plenty of courses of action to take. There were outstanding people to interview, of course. I would need to talk with Dawn, the woman who helped Gillian in the tanning salon. I wanted to speak with Thi and the other woman who pretended to get their nails forever done. Gillian had provided me with their information.

There was canvassing to do, also. I should connect with the neighboring businesses and walk through the mobile home park behind Gillian's building. I'd have to develop a ruse to achieve that. Otherwise, I might do more harm and shine a light on Gillian's illegal activity.

The same thing could be said of Double G. I'd met Gary Gaspar when I helped resolve Remo's problem earlier in the year, and we'd parted as professionals—at least, I hoped so. However, Gaspar wasn't the type of acquaintance I could call up and ask if he was involved with a robbery attempt of a marijuana grow. What if he didn't know anything, and I alerted him to it?

Gillian already had enough trouble with the crew who hit her place, and the Wasted Souls were now inside the hen house. If I brought Double G around, she might as well pack it in and go home.

All of that could wait, though. Right now, I had a favor to pay back, and it was one I couldn't put off for long. Not because I couldn't do it later, but because that's not how a person repaid Deacon.

***

"Cutler."

"Hey, man."

Tremaine Brown pulled open the door to his home and stepped back. I held the screen so that it wouldn't clatter. He shut the door behind me.

We sat in the living room—him on the sofa, me in a heavily worn armchair. Between us was a low coffee table. On the shelf underneath were books about Martin Luther King Jr., Malcolm X, and the Selma-to-Montgomery marches.

Even though it was still bright outside, the curtains were drawn. A single lamp was lit. Crystal baubles dangled from the shade. Two box fans sat at opposite sides of the room and blew warm air toward each other.

A home entertainment center stood next to the nearest wall. The TV was silent. VHS tapes were neatly lined up. They had titles like *The Color Purple*, *Do the Right Thing*, and *In the Heat of the Night*.

Photographs of Tremaine and Dontari Brown as younger boys were carefully placed about the room.

The Brown family lived in the Perry District. The neighborhood was walking distance from downtown and a recent discovery of local hipsters. With the influx of younger residents, a strip of retail business on Perry Street was under change. A couple of older buildings had recently been reborn as restaurants. It was still too early to tell if the change would hold.

"Is your mother home?" I asked. I'd never met Rosemary Brown.

"She's working." As an afterthought, Tremaine added. "Up at the hospital. Swing shift."

"I didn't know. Deacon never told me what she did."

"Why would he? My mother's job is none of your fucking business."

"Easy, man."

Tremaine stood, and his face pinched with anger. "Why do you keep calling me 'man?' Is that your modern way of calling me 'boy?'"

My jaw clenched, and my ears warmed. I fought the urge to stand, too.

Tremaine's fists balled, and he leaned forward slightly. "Huh?"

"I was trying to be cool," I said evenly.

"You aren't."

"That's what my daughter tells me." I held up an apologetic hand. "I'm sorry. It's just a word I use, but I won't use it again. Can we start over?"

Tremaine sighed. "Listen, man." He caught himself using the same word and smirked. "Let's not do this. Why don't we pretend we had this conversation, and you go about your business? Deacon can tell my mother that he did his best and—"

I shook my head. "I'm not going to lie to Deacon. Either we talk, or we don't. I don't give a shit either way."

Tremaine studied me for a bit, then flopped back into the sofa.

"What's your mother do?"

He eyed me. "Why do you care?"

"Just making conversation. Trying to be nice."

His smirk faded. "She's a nurse."

I glanced around. "Is Dontari here?"

"You see him?"

"When's he coming back?"

"How would I know?"

"I thought you might care about him seeing me."

Tremaine waved a hand. "You think I'm worried about that? My little brother talks to who he talks to, and I don't care."

"How much time have we got until he gets back?"

"Don't be a bitch, Cutler. You got as much time to say what you've got to say." Tremaine leaned forward and rested his elbows on his knees. "Start talking or start walking. I got shit to do."

"Deacon brags you up. Says you're smart and talented."

"This is why you came here?" He mimed jerking off. "I don't need an ego stroke from you."

"That's not what I'm giving. Deacon thinks you're wasting your future by getting involved with the Dead Boys."

Tremaine clucked his tongue. "I'm not wasting anything."

"From what I understand, you're doing it to protect your brother."

He waved his hand. "We're not having this discussion."

I pointed to a picture on the entertainment system—a younger Tremaine in a green baseball uniform. "Who were you playing for?"

He didn't answer.

"Looks like you were in junior high."

Tremaine shrugged a single shoulder. "Why do you care?"

I scooted to the edge of my chair. "I played right field at that age."

His lip curled. "The hell you doing, Cutler?"

My brow furrowed.

"You think you can come into my house and give me a little song and dance about how you played the game, too? We're never gonna connect over baseball. This ain't *Field of Dreams*, Cutler. You ain't Kevin Costner, and I'm not James Earl Jones."

My eyes flicked to the VHS tapes wondering if it would be there amongst the other movies that featured great black actors. I didn't find it. I was surprised the kid knew the film and who starred in it. My gaze returned to Tremaine. I thought about abandoning baseball, but my gut told me to stay the course.

"I sat on the bench," I said, "I could catch and throw, but I was never any good at hitting."

Tremaine walked over and picked up the photograph. "Second base," he muttered. "I batted cleanup." His thumb rubbed the edge of the frame.

"So, you *were* good."

He nodded and studied the photograph intently.

"Do you play anymore?"

Tremaine's gaze hardened, and he put the photograph back. "I put childish things away. That's from that bible my mother loves so much." He sat on the edge of the coffee table near me. "Truce."

I lifted an eyebrow.

Tremaine patted his chest. "I'm sorry for being a dick."

Just a moment ago, he'd referenced his mother's bible. She'd obviously had an impact on his character. The forces in his life seemed to be battling for control.

"I appreciate what you're doing for Deacon," Tremaine said. "I'm serious. The man put you in a no-win situation, yet you still came. I respect that. I doubt if I would do that for him."

I thought he might, but I kept it to myself.

"The old man has had a soft spot for my mother since I've known him. She adores him the way my grandmother adores her cats."

Tremaine saying 'adore' was like Remo saying 'smart cookie.' It sounded odd. It was probably Rosemary

Brown's vernacular, and Tremaine adopted it for the things she described in those terms.

"My mother's never going to love the fat man in the way he loves her."

"Maybe he knows that."

His eyes narrowed. "If he knows that, why waste his time on her? I mean, my mom is my mom, and I love her and all—" Tremaine held a hand over his heart. "—but if a woman wasn't giving me the time of day, I'd kick her fat ass to the curb and move on. Plenty of them in the sea, and Deacon isn't the type of man to be picky about it."

"Men do a lot of things for women who don't love them." It may have been the most truthful thing I'd ever said.

"Well, not me," Tremaine said confidently. "No woman is going to push me around."

"You're young."

He smirked.

"And maybe Deacon isn't doing this for her. Maybe he's doing this for you."

Tremaine barked a single laugh. "Bullshit."

"Why?"

"He's nice to me, so he can get to her. It's the game. Everybody uses everybody."

"Deacon cares about you."

Tremaine rubbed his hands together and remained silent.

"He wants you to achieve something more than the gang."

He scowled. "Well, he can stop worrying about that. Dontari and me, we're with the Dead Boys, and nothing will change that."

"Maybe—"

He hopped to his feet and towered over me. He pulled his shoulders back and clenched his fists. "Listen to what

I said, Cutler—nothing will change that." He pointed out of the house. "Not some fat man wanting to play white savior—" Now, he pointed at me. "And not some broken-down former cop with a case of white guilt."

I slowly stood.

"Deacon is dying," I said.

He rolled his eyes. "We're all dying, Cutler, or didn't you know? Every second we're all one heartbeat closer to the end. Deacon's one of the lucky ones. He's lived a long time." Tremaine's gaze darted to the clock. "Ten minutes. You think you've been talking long enough? Because I do."

"It's been more than enough."

"My thoughts exactly." His face flattened.

Tremaine followed me to the door. I turned back to him.

"What do you know about drugs?" I asked.

"For real?" He laughed. "You come to save me, but now you want to score. Motherfucker, your white guilt must have whiplash."

"Are the Dead Boys involved with them?"

He stepped back. "If you're going to preach—"

I lifted a hand to interrupt him. "Where do you get your supply?"

"I'm not telling you shit. Are you some sort of narc or something?" He looked me up and down. "You wearing a wire?"

I lifted my shirt. "Pat me down if you want."

Tremaine took another step back. "What are you after, Cutler?"

"It's not what you think."

"Better convince me quick, or I'm gonna think this was all a ruse to find out how our network is set up."

Adore. Ruse. They were only words but not the typical choice of a teenager. Deacon was right. Tremaine was smart.

I asked, "Do you know the local suppliers?"

"You mean our competition?" His brow furrowed. "Depends. What product are we talking about?"

"Weed."

"Weed?" He smirked. "Oh Christ, Cutler. What decade did you crawl out of?"

"What should I call it?"

"Anything but weed. Trees, chronic, gasper—"

"Gaspar?"

"You know." He mimed inhaling on a joint in small bursts. He spoke while holding a breath deep in his lungs. "A gasper."

It wasn't what I thought. "So, do you know any of the growers in town?"

"You could throw a baseball and hit a grower. Every high school kid has a plant in their basement."

"I'm talking a grower in the county." I tried to keep Gillian's location as vague as possible. "They've got a nice set-up. Growing a hundred plants essentially in the open."

"Bullshit—a hundred plants. There's no way that's happening in the open."

"You haven't heard of it?"

"It's not real," Tremaine said. He dismissed my question with a wave. "Some pot head fantasy."

"Maybe it's real, and you're too low-level to know about it."

He rolled his eyes. "Quit trying to goad me, Cutler, and get outta my house."

Goad. There was another one. It was hard not to like the kid.

When I returned home, I grabbed Corporal and his graying tennis ball. We walked across the street to the park. I threw the ball as hard as I could for thirty minutes, and he brought it back

Eventually, he trotted out, collected the ball, and sat.

"Bring it back," I hollered.

When he settled into the grass, I lifted my hands.

"What are you doing? Let's go!"

Corporal dropped the ball and panted.

"Yeah, okay, I get it." I headed for home. "Fall in!" I yelled.

The dog picked up the ball and scampered toward me.

Back inside the house, he lapped water from his bowl.

I checked the messages on my landline. There was only one.

"Cutler, you know who this is. We need to talk."

There was no number or address given, but that didn't matter. I indeed knew who it was. The voice was hard to forget—Double G.

I deleted the message.

It was Monday night. All I wanted was to eat something and chill out for a couple of hours before going to bed.

There were burritos in the freezer that I could microwave, but that didn't sound good tonight.

In the fridge were a few eggs. I thought about scrambling them, but that seemed like too much work.

In a cabinet, I rummaged through various canned foods. There was chili, corned beef hash, and several types of soup. The house was warm, so heating a stove to make dinner didn't sound appealing. I selected a can, opened it, and grabbed a spoon. Then I sat at my desk and turned on the nearby TV.

For the next ten minutes, I ate cold chili from a can while I watched a rerun of *M*A*S*H*. Hawkeye and Trapper John couldn't remove the worry that Double G placed in me.

Why was he calling? I had wanted to see him and ask if he knew Gillian, but his wanting to see me was worrisome. When I finished the chili, I tossed my spoon into the can and set it aside.

After *M*A*S*H*, a reality TV show started. I couldn't understand this craze. First, it was fake. Reality doesn't have cameras set up everywhere, nor contestants playing for some contrived prize. Second, if I wanted reality, I'd turn off the television.

That's what I did.

As I stood, the cell phone rang. I answered it.

"Two nights in a row," I said.

"Can you come over?" Stacy asked. "Like now?" She didn't sound like her usual self.

I glanced out the front window. The sun was still up. I never went to Stacy's while it was light out. As far as our relationship was concerned, I could have been a vampire.

"Isn't it a little early? Aren't the kids still awake?"

"Please, John. Can you come over?"

"Yeah, sure. You okay?"

"Just get here soon."

I picked up the empty can. The spoon rattled as it swirled around inside. "I'll head over now."

"See you in a bit."

She hung up.

I stared at the phone for a minute. "Well, okay then."

***

Stacy answered the door before I could knock.

"The kids are playing in their room. Be quiet."

She pulled me inside and gently closed the door. We tiptoed to her room. I sat on the edge of the bed and watched her. Stacy locked her bedroom door.

When she turned, she stayed out of reach. I didn't try to touch her. This was clearly not that type of visit, and I wasn't thick-headed enough to try and make it something different.

I figured she was about to tell me something concerning her ex-husband. As far as Stacy went, she was primarily drama-free except when it came to her former spouse. She didn't talk about him a lot, but it was with terms like *manipulative*, *angry*, and *bastard* when she did. I heard a lot about him when we first met, but she'd generally been silent on the topic since then.

Stacy said, "Tanya knows about us."

I figured it wrong but didn't see the problem. "So?"

Her eyes bulged. "Are you kidding me? My sister shows up here in a rage, makes a big, embarrassing scene in front of my kids, and all you say is 'so?' I thought she was going to hit me. She was so mad that I had to shove her out of the house. My own sister."

"Was she drunk?"

"Is the pope Catholic?"

I fell back to my elbows and watched her. "You could have told me this over the phone."

Stacy paced in front of the bed. "I thought this was something we should do face-to-face."

My shrug was limited due to the weight on my elbows.

She stopped and eyed me. "You're not worried?"

"What's she going to do?"

"She could come to your place. She could make another scene."

"She's not going to come to my house," I said. "Not now, and definitely not drunk."

"Why not?"

"That would show weakness, and she wouldn't do that. Not to me, and probably not to any guy."

Stacy's eyes narrowed.

"You have nothing to worry about."

She moved toward the edge of the bed. "But what if she shows up tomorrow when she's not drunk? Do I have to be worried then?"

"No."

"You're sure?"

I nodded once. "I'm more than sure. There's nothing there."

Stacy climbed onto the bed and sat on my lap. I remained reclined on my elbows.

"If anything happens between you two—"

"It won't," I said.

"Promise?"

"I promise."

She kissed me.

"Mom?" a little girl said just before the doorknob jiggled.

We both looked toward it.

"Mom?"

"What, Hailey?"

"What are you doing in there?"

Stacy eyed me. "Nothing."

"Who are you talking to?"

"No one."

"I heard you talking."

"That was the TV."

A little hand slipped underneath the door and ran along its edge. Fingers wriggled as if hoping to find something to grab.

Stacy said, "Go to your room, Hailey. I'll be there in a minute."

"What are you doing?"

"*Now*, Hailey."

The hand withdrew from under the door.

Stacy faced me. "Where were we?"

"Why don't I take off and—"

"Where are you going?"

"You need to take care of them."

"And?" She slipped off the edge of the bed. "You stay here. I'll be back." Stacy snatched the remote from the nightstand and tossed it onto my lap. "Watch some TV."

"I don't want—"

"Or take a nap. I don't care. But you're not leaving."

"I'm not?"

Stacy pointed at me. "My sister is upset, which means one thing. She's going to be on the prowl, and I'm about to mark my territory."

She cracked the door open slightly and peered into the hallway. Then she slipped out and closed the door behind her.

I considered the remote for a moment before setting it back on the nightstand.

For a time, I stared at the ceiling and considered the situation.

Tanya was bound to find out about Stacy and me sooner or later. I'm not sure why it mattered what I did with Stacy, as I was only ever a pressure relief valve for Tanya. But jealousy was a dangerous thing. It turned people inside out and made them take reckless actions. As a police officer, I responded to many domestic violence calls where the green-eyed monster was the root cause.

In fact, I had experienced jealousy so powerful that it started me down a path that cost me that same police officer job. I understood the ugly power of that emotion. It wasn't something to be trifled with.

My mind drifted to the problem I dealt with during the day. I thought about Gillian and her setup. I had to hand it to her. She'd set it up in an ingenious way—the tanning salon to hide power consumption and the screen printer for the chemical smell. Maybe the nail salon contributed to the chemical smell, too. And all three businesses laundered her money.

Could anyone be jealous of what she built?

Not her employees—at least, the two I talked with. They seemed to appreciate her and what she did for them. And I doubted the go-betweens she sold to would have been jealous. If the product was good, the price fair, and the supply reliable, they would want to keep it coming.

But Double G's name came up a couple of times now. And he'd left me a message. If he somehow knew about her grow, could he be jealous of it? I didn't know the man well enough to determine such a thing. But if money could be made robbing the grow, I could fully see him doing such a thing.

What about Remo? He didn't seem the envious type. Instead, he seemed content to keep selling dope like he'd been doing since high school. What a life.

A thought came to me, but voices and footsteps in the hallway interrupted it.

"Hailey, what are you doing?" Stacy was outside the bedroom door.

"I want to sleep in your bed."

"You have to sleep in your own."

Hailey whined, "But I want to sleep in *yours*."

"Tomorrow night."

"Why not tonight?"

"Because I said."

"Aww."

The footsteps walked back down the hallway.

I returned to the thought I'd just had. Remo left his previous dealer to start working with Gillian. Maybe there'd been some resentment there when he left. Do drug dealers feel jealousy like a scorned lover? Did Remo leave his former supplier without any repercussions?

I would have to meet with Remo in the morning to find out.

The door to the bedroom opened, and Stacy stepped inside. She quietly closed the door, then locked it.

"You stayed awake," she said.

"Uh-huh."

Stacy moved toward the bed. "So that you know, you never get to go back to Tanya."

"I would never consider such a thing."

She pulled her shirt over her head. "Let's make sure of that."

Chapter 7

I left Stacy's in the middle of the night and woke up in my own bed. After a shower and a shave, the dog and I went across the street to the park.

The sun was up, the sky was bright blue, and the temperature must have already been in the mid-eighties. Even though the sprinklers ran in the early morning, the grass was already dry. A group of teenagers was on the nearby basketball courts. The pool wasn't open yet.

I threw the dirty tennis ball as hard as I could. Corporal chased it to the far end of the park. We played for almost thirty minutes before he had enough. He picked it up one final time, took a couple of steps toward me, then sat.

"You done?" I hollered.

The dog lay on his belly, and the ball fell from his mouth. He panted and watched me.

Across the street from the park, a black Chrysler 300 pulled to the curb in front of my house. On the far side of the car, the passenger door opened. A thin white man in sunglasses stepped out and looked over the hood. He eyed me for a moment, then jerked his head—a silent command for me to come home. Then the man settled back into the car.

"Shit," I muttered.

I had planned to return home anyway but doing so now seemed wrong. I'm not sure anyone liked being ordered around—I especially didn't. I thought about staying longer in the park for a moment, but that wouldn't help my situation. It would likely do the opposite.

"Fall in!" I yelled.

Corporal snatched up the ball and ran to me. We then walked side-by-side toward the house. I thought about showing good faith and taking a path in front of the Chrysler, but that was for the movies. We hurried behind the car and up to my house. I opened the door and let Corporal inside. He turned back and waited for me.

"At ease," I said.

The dog immediately went for his water bowl. I closed the door and moved to the edge of the steps.

Gary Gaspar exited his car again. He wore a short-sleeved black shirt, black slacks, and black loafers. His dark hair was cut short, and his sunglasses were made of expensive black plastic.

The only thing on him that wasn't black was the Super Bowl ring he wore on the middle finger of his left hand. Double G had never played professional football. Gaspar told me he'd gotten the ring from a former player when the guy defaulted on a loan repayment. Now, Gaspar wore the ring to symbolize what someone could lose if they failed to pay their dues. It might have all been bullshit, but the truth was hard to find with Double G.

"Cutler," he said.

"G." Gaspar preferred to be called that or even Double G. It didn't take a genius to understand the effect of branding.

I descended the stairs and headed toward him. He didn't bother moving toward me. Everything was a power play with him. Gaspar had left the passenger door open so his driver could hear us. I leaned down and eyed Trace. He lifted his chin toward me, and I returned the gesture.

An old Chevy Monza drove by. Its engine rumbled, and its exhaust pipe rattled.

Gaspar watched the car until it drove by the community center at the west end of the block. Then he looked in the opposite direction down Spofford Avenue. "You need some new digs."

"This suits me fine."

His lip curled. "Haven't you ever heard about not shitting where you eat?"

I stayed quiet. There was no reason to argue about where my office was located.

"Your name came up, Cutler."

"In what way?" I asked.

"In conjunction with Remo. He's back in town again, but you already knew that."

I refused to look away and show any weakness. I remained silent.

"Last time you two got together, it cost me forty-eight hundred."

"You're remembering it wrong."

The driver's door opened, and Trace stepped out. He had thick shoulders and no neck. Trace rested his forearms on the car's roof and glared at me. "The hell you say, Cutler?"

Gaspar raised a hand to hold off his guy. "It's okay."

"But he said—"

"I know what he said. He's just pissing in the wind, Trace. This is Cutler, after all. His bark is worse than his bite."

"You got that right." Trace slid back into the car and pulled the door shut.

Gaspar slipped his sunglasses from his face and pointed them at me. "Why don't you tell me how I *should* remember things, Cutler?"

"I solved a problem for you and Remo."

Double G stared unblinkingly at me.

"Doesn't that sound nicer?"

"You're an asshole, Cutler."

I spread my hands apart in a non-threatening manner. "C'mon, Double G. I'm a peacemaker. That should count for something."

"This ain't the United Nations."

"Remo wasn't a specialist. You knew that when you brought him in, but you still chose to move forward with the job."

Gaspar put his sunglasses on. "He was the lookout, for Christ's sake."

"The job still came off okay."

"Despite Remo's screw-up."

I clasped my hands and let them loosely hang in front of my body. "Nobody's saying he did his part perfectly, but he still deserved to be paid. You're not here to renegotiate that deal, are you?"

"I'm going on your word that there was never a video."

"Cross my heart."

Gaspar's lip curled. "Hope to die?"

"I've got to stop saying that."

He pointed at my house. "What's stopping us from going in there and making sure there's no video?" Gaspar now pointed at my head with his thumb and two fingers.

I lifted my hands and surrendered to his imaginary gun. "There was never a video, G. And if there was, do you think I'd be stupid enough to keep it at my house?"

He lowered his hand and holstered his thumb and fingers.

"I never asked for more than what was promised," I said. "And I never threatened nor tried to extort you. As far as I am concerned, our business was concluded."

Gaspar's eyes narrowed.

"That should show you something about the person I am."

He opened his mouth to say something but slowly closed it. Gaspar's jaw muscles flexed before his tongue darted out to wet his lips. "Tell me this, Cutler. What *are* you and Remo doing together now?"

"Nothing."

"You see, I don't believe that. Word is he's back in town a minute, and you two meet up. People said you two were all friendly like and I want to know why because the last that I heard, he took off with your fee."

The only time Remo and I had been together was at his place. We weren't friendly in his backyard. Someone could have seen us talking when I left his apartment. He followed me down the steps and into the driveway. We shared a laugh about me pulling him out of the window. Then I left.

How had anyone seen us in that brief amount of time? And how had they known to contact Gaspar?

I'd forgotten a rule of the street. There were eyes everywhere, and everyone knew when someone had a cross to bear. Those two things could lead someone to call Gaspar and report that he'd seen us together.

"Remo wanted to apologize," I said.

"For running off with your fee?"

"Among other things."

Gaspar's eyes narrowed. "He make good?"

I was on dangerous ground here. If I told him that Remo did, there would be questions about where the money came from. Remo had the money months ago, but he'd taken off to Mexico. It was highly unlikely he would return with enough to pay me off.

And I couldn't reveal that I had been paid off by someone else. That would send Gaspar down the rabbit hole of asking questions. He'd know better than to try getting answers from me. Instead, he'd go directly to Remo.

"He gave me a couple hundred," I lied.

"He owed you twenty-four."

I nodded. "He's going to pay me off as he earns."

"And you're okay with that?"

"What other choice do I have?"

Gaspar smirked. "You should have broken his thumbs."

"He can't earn with broken thumbs. I needed the money more."

He turned slightly. "All right, Cutler. If that's all it was about, all right. Just make sure you and Remo aren't going to try and get in any more of my business."

There was something in the way he said it that pricked my ears. It was that slight tingle of suspicion that I used to get on the street. "What business are we getting into, G?"

Gaspar motioned toward the car. "You want I should call Trace out here and remind you to keep those kinds of questions to yourself?"

"No, I'm good. I can do without that reminding."

He reached for his door.

"Hey, G?"

Gaspar looked over his shoulder.

"You know much about the dope game?"

He slowly turned back to me. Suspicion clouded his eyes. "Why?"

"There's a grower out in the county."

Gaspar frowned. "Where?"

"Doesn't matter."

His frown morphed into a smirk. "I'd imagine there's a lot of growers in the county. Bunch of mouth breathers and paste eaters living in the unincorporated land."

"Somebody tried to hit it."

His frown returned with a vengeance. Something in his body language caused the driver's door to open, and Trace climbed out. "You think I'm involved?"

"I'm just asking."

Gaspar stepped forward, and Trace hurried around the front of the car.

"I'm not behind every bit of criminal activity in this town, Cutler." His finger thumped my chest. "You should be careful where you throw those kinds of accusations."

I raised my hands mostly in deference but also to have them ready to fight Gaspar and Trace if need be. The security man now stood off to my right.

"I apologize," I said. "I was just asking."

"Why even bring it up? You mixed up in it somehow?"

I thought about telling Gaspar some version of the truth but thought I'd already said too much. I needed to get him off the scent. "There was a rumor about a heist," I said. "And I thought of you."

"Well, get it out of your head." His eyes flicked to his security man. "And if you can't, Trace can help."

I noticed the big man shifting his stance from the corner of my eye.

"I'm good," I said.

Gaspar nodded. "Keep it that way." He stepped back. "And don't bring my name up around shit like that. Understand?"

"Yeah, I got it."

Trace backpedaled his way toward the Chrysler and dropped into the driver's seat when he neared it.

With a final shake of his head, Gaspar turned to his car and settled into the passenger seat. Before the door slammed closed, the Chrysler pulled from the curb.

***

Inside my house, I placed a call to Remo. He'd given me his new number the last time we talked. After several rings, it went to voice mail. I left a message, but that didn't satisfy me since I now knew where he lived.

I drove to his above-garage apartment—I'd done enough walking on Sunday.

A cream-colored Volvo station wagon was parked in the driveway. I walked by it, passed through the small chain link fence, then proceeded up the stairs to Remo's apartment. I knocked.

When he didn't answer, I knocked again. This time harder.

The windows were too high from the stairs for me to peer into. I jiggled the doorknob, but it was locked.

The back door to the main house opened, and Elva Lightly peered out. It looked as if I might have woken her. Her long hair was disheveled, and her wrinkled face appeared mashed as if she might have slept facing down. She wore a dingy white t-shirt and green shorts.

"The hell you doing?" she rasped.

"Looking for Remo."

She angrily flicked her hand. "Take that bullshit elsewhere."

I started down the steps. "Any idea where he might be?"

Elva stepped back. "Working people trying to sleep" is all I caught before the door slammed shut. The windows in the house shook.

I called Remo's phone once more. When he didn't answer, I left another voice mail.

"Remo, this is John Cutler. Second time. Call me."

***

I drove east toward Gillian's building. I stopped at a Taco Time and bought two breakfast burritos and a cup of coffee along the way. I held off eating until I arrived at the mobile home park that sat directly behind Sunshine Smiles.

The wooden sign for Park Estates desperately needed updating. A painted park-like setting once adorned the panel, but most of it had faded or flaked off courtesy of the drastic changes in weather that this region experienced. The only thing readily visible was the park's name in blocky once-white letters, which were now mostly gray, and a telephone number that someone had spray-painted a red line through. Weeds sprouted around the legs of the support posts. A dirty diaper and an old tire lay nearby in faded tree bark—both discarded victims of long-ago blow-outs.

I drove along a winding road until I came to the back of the park. I found a spot where I could see the rear of Gillian's building and parked. Resting between the exit doors of the tanning salon and the screen-printing shop was a large piece of plywood. It hadn't been there yesterday.

Five trailers were nearby—three on the south side of the road closest to the tanning salon and its sister businesses.

Before enjoying my breakfast, I rolled down my window. I wanted to know what I could smell from here. The chemical stink from Dandy Designs was not noticeable. The only thing I could easily detect were the extra onions I requested in my burritos. I unwrapped one and took a bite. Like a kid, I happily ate—the breakfast burrito had eggs, sausage, and tater tots in it. It was the tater tots that did it for me.

I didn't notice a breeze as I sat in the truck, but it must have shifted because that horrible rotten smell from the rendering plant wafted inside. I grimaced and hurriedly closed my window.

For a moment, I considered finishing my breakfast. The rotten odor was trapped in the cab now. I wrapped up the remaining burrito and put it to the side. I'd eat it and its companion later. The tater tots wouldn't go to waste.

I climbed out of the cab and was greeted by the putrid stench again.

"Damn," I muttered.

"Potent this morning, ain't it?"

A woman approached with a yellow cat on a leather leash. The woman was in her late forties but looked surprisingly like Elva Lightly had—mashed-in face, dingy white t-shirt, and green shorts. She was even barefooted, which startled me since the Park Estate's asphalt roadway was crumbled and covered in little stones.

"The rendering plant," I said, stating the obvious.

"Tuesdays is always the worst. Not sure why." She stopped near me and studied me without reservation. She pinched her nose and said in a distorted voice, "Most days, you get used to it, but not on days like today. What agency is you with?"

"Excuse me?"

She pointed at me with her elbow and then motioned to my truck. Her warped voice continued due to the pinched nose. "You's all dressed up like you's going to church, and you got yourself that new truck. I'm guessing you's with the state."

I wore a black t-shirt, blue jeans, and boots. My truck was almost ten years old, and the only thing going for it was that it was recently washed.

Before I could respond, she asked, "What kind of inspection is you doing?"

"I'm not an inspector."

The breeze stopped, and the odor of death vanished. I lifted my nose and searched for a chemical smell or a whiff of marijuana but didn't get either.

The woman let go of her nose and wriggled it for a moment. "Wait for it."

I eyed her.

"That wind will bring it around once more. Count on it." She leaned her head back and looked down her nose. "This place ain't for sale again, is it? Tell me you isn't one of them real estate types." She seemed agitated and ready to fight.

"Not me."

"Phew. Thank God. I can't stand them types. Always so arrogant like they's better than us."

"Do you get a lot of agencies out here?"

"Oh, sure." She waved her free hand about. "They's always inspecting one thing or another. Don't know why. Nothin' ever improves round here."

"What do they inspect?"

She tugged on the cat's leash. It wasn't trying to walk away. She looked up in sudden irritation. "What's your name again?"

"I never said."

Her eyes narrowed with distrust.

"My name is John." I extended my hand. "What's yours?"

"Xavia. And before you ask, it's my real name."

"I didn't say it wasn't."

She slowly looked down at the cat. "I didn't make it up." It was said without much conviction.

"Wouldn't matter if you did."

Her gaze snapped up to me. "That's right. It wouldn't. Do you like it?"

"I like it fine. What kind of agencies are out here?"

"All kinds," Xavia said. "They's always got them fancy trucks like you do."

"Do the police ever come out here?"

"They come out sometimes, yeah." Her eyes went toward the park's east end, and she hollered, "Because some people don't know how to drink quietly like goddamned adults!" Xavia tugged on the cat's leash again. This time it had tried to wander off. "And sometimes I think those cops come out just to drive through and see what's what."

"Are there problems going on here besides the loud drinking?"

"Not really, no. The cops prolly wanna make sure everyone knows they's watching." She pointed two fingers at her eyes, then at me, then she scanned the park with them. Then she nodded with satisfaction. "That's how they do things."

"Do you like that?" I asked.

"Cops keeping an eye on things? Don't bother me none." Her brow furrowed. "You never said how come you's out here."

I glanced around the park. "I'm looking for a place to live."

She frowned. "This don't seem the type of place for you. Not with the stink and the noise and the weirdos." She leaned in as if sharing a secret. "There's some strange types here. You should see them." Xavia straightened. "Why you could live someplace else, I imagine. Not unless…"

"Unless what?"

I expected her to ask if I wanted to buy and flip a home. I hadn't heard of anyone doing that with mobile homes, but maybe that was a thing. Xavia hunched slightly and looked around in a conspiratorial fashion. "You ain't a loud drinker, are you?"

I shook my head.

"Maybe you done something and need to hide out. This would be a good place to do it."

"I haven't done anything."

"Are you sure? I mean, if you did, you can tell me. I can keep a secret."

"Nothing. I promise."

She stood upright again, but now disappointment filled her eyes. The cat wandered away from her. "Most folks who live here have either done something, or they got something wrong with them. So, what's wrong with you?"

"Nothing."

"You're a secretive type," she said, "I get it. Me? I got issues. You probably couldn't tell, but I do." She tugged on the cat again. Then she pointed at a series of trailers behind me. "That one's afraid to leave his trailer, that one's hiding from her ex-husband, and that one thinks she's Jesus." Xavia smiled. "But she'll give you Ritz crackers and grape juice on Sunday, so there's that."

I'm glad I hadn't told her any of my secrets. "How long have most people been here?"

"Years."

"Anyone new move in?"

She shook her head. "Not in a long time. Last one was a couple years ago, I think. I might be wrong, but it's been a long time for sure. People move in, but they don't move out." Xavia cocked her head. "Wasn't there an advertisement for something that went like that?"

I sniffed the air again. I still hadn't smelled the chemicals from the screen-printing shop or any marijuana odor. I didn't want to ask Xavia if she ever noticed those two scents and put the thought into her head. I'd found out enough by being there.

She chuckled. "The roach motel. That's it. People move in, but they don't move out."

"Thanks for your help," I said and stepped toward my truck.

"You's leaving?"

"Yeah."

"You decide against moving here?"

I nodded.

"Probably for the best. You'd probably fall in love with me, and then where would we be?" She tugged on the leash and pulled the cat in her direction. Xavia wandered off toward the north.

Chapter 8

Dawn Naylor rested her elbows on the tanning salon's sales counter. We'd already gotten the introductions out of the way. She was in her late twenties with bottled blond hair, brown eyebrows, and green eyes. Her tanned skin was flawless, and a lot of it was shown as she wore a tight pair of shorts and a midriff shirt.

Gnarls Barkley's "Crazy" played through the salon's radio.

I motioned toward the new pane of glass. "They replaced the window."

Dawn's gaze narrowed. "You're really a private eye?"

"Investigator. Yeah."

"You don't look like one."

"How are they supposed to look?"

Her eyes traveled my length. "I don't know, but not like you."

She disapproved of the appearance that Xavia seemed to think looked professional. Maybe I should heed Dawn's opinion. I didn't change much about my daily outfit except the color of my t-shirts.

"You work here part-time," I said.

Dawn pushed up from her elbows to her hands. "That's right."

"Not enough to live on, I suspect. You work elsewhere?"

She shook her head. "I don't need to. I live with my folks."

"Yeah?"

"Don't be a dick."

I lifted an apologetic hand. "I wasn't."

"It's not because I want to, believe me. Places are expensive. Plus, I got other reasons for working here."

"The trees, you mean?"

Dawn scoffed. "Trees? Who told you to say that?"

"What's wrong with it?"

She stepped around the counter and gave me a good going-over. I could now see the white sandals she wore. "Saying trees makes you sound like a narc. Weed or dope is more your speed, grandpa."

"I'm not that much older than you."

"Coulda fooled me." Her head bobbed from side to side. "You act old enough to be my father."

The comment bothered me. She was clearly challenging me. She was an attractive woman who showed a lot of skin. In another situation, I might have smiled and made some small talk in a vain effort to get her to like me. But today, I was professional—there was a double fee at stake.

I rubbed my chin. "So, the weed—that's one of the reasons you work here?"

Dawn's smile was filled with the thrill of victory. "I've never smoked it once. I don't want that stuff messing with my mind. And I don't drink for the same reason. Plus, that booze makes you fat."

"Your reason is free tanning, then?"

Dawn shrugged a single shoulder. "What if it is?"

"The beds are low-pressure. I figured someone as tanned as you switched out now and then. Maybe you're getting the extra sun from outside, but what do you do in the winter?"

"Maybe you *are* a private eye." Dawn leaned a single elbow on the counter and crossed one ankle around the back of the other. Her head bobbled a little more this time. It was all an effect to deliver a message, and it worked. I felt better about myself.

The song on the radio ended, and a commercial for a cell phone company started.

"So, that's why you work here?"

Her brow furrowed. "You really wanna know?" Dawn's lips briefly pursed, then she shrugged a single shoulder. "I can't drive."

"This is walking distance from your home?"

She nodded.

My eyes flicked to her sandals and painted toenails. She hadn't walked far. I pointed toward the back of the building. "You live in the mobile home park?"

"Aw, hell no." She quickly lifted an embarrassed hand. "I'm sorry. I didn't mean for it to come off that way. It's just that—" Dawn sighed. "I wouldn't live back there."

"Why not?"

"I got higher standards than that."

"But you didn't walk far in those sandals. Not unless they just gave your toenails a touch-up over at Naomi Nail."

"I have a pair of Vans behind the counter. You keep impressing me, Mr. Private Eye. You got a thing for feet or something?"

Dopamine spiked through my system, and I felt stupid for it. I lifted my chin toward her but didn't say anything.

She straightened and crossed her arms around her midsection. Almost as soon as her forearms touched her exposed skin, she relaxed and dragged her fingers across her flat stomach. Her hands rested on her hips, and her eyes met mine. I got the feeling Dawn wasn't a woman used to having her signals ignored.

Several beats passed, and she still hadn't answered my question.

"You were saying?" I prompted. "About why you don't drive."

"It's embarrassing. It's not the thing I talk about with men I've just met."

"You already called me grandpa. Think of me like that."

Dawn's face soured, and she assessed me once more. After a moment, a lascivious grin appeared. "You don't look like my grandfather."

"Let's stop." I pointed at the cameras that hung from the ceiling. "Gillian isn't paying either of us to hook up."

Her face darkened. "I was just playing around."

"It's confusing to a guy like me. It could make me do a lot of stupid things."

An eyebrow lifted, and her demeanor changed once more. It was as if she scored a point in the game that men and women had been locked in since time began. Happy that she notched one for her side, Dawn moved behind the counter. "I've got…" Her head bounced as she sought for a word. She settled on, "Problems."

"That's why you don't drink or smoke."

"As my doctors say, I don't need anything to affect my sense of reality."

Dawn tried to sound tough, but a scared little girl lurked in those words.

"How'd you meet Gillian?" I asked.

She tapped the counter. "I came in right after she opened the business. I might have even been her first customer." Dawn tilted her head knowingly. "Her first *real* customer. I kept coming back, and we started talking. She's pretty cool. After a while, we became friends."

"Have you told anyone about her business?"

"No."

"Maybe you didn't realize you did it."

"I said no. I know how to keep a secret."

"All I'm saying is that—"

Dawn smacked the counter. "I haven't said shit to anyone, and you can put me on a lie detector if you want. Gillian is my friend, and I wouldn't do her like that."

I lifted my hands in a calming manner. "All right."

She stepped away from the counter and crossed her arms over her stomach. This time she didn't move them away. She averted her eyes from my gaze. "If there's nothing else—"

There wasn't a need for her to finish the thought.

"Thank you for your time, Dawn."

She nodded but still didn't look at me.

I turned, pushed open the exit door, and headed to my truck.

***

Thi Nguyen lived in a duplex on Wellesley Avenue. I found it courtesy of an address Gillian had texted earlier in the morning. I pulled onto nearby Cook Street and parked. Wellesley is a heavily traveled east-west arterial in north Spokane. Cars and trucks zipped by as I walked toward Thi's place.

The duplex was a brown and orange split-level affair with one unit above the other rather than side by side. It was built sometime in the seventies when it was probably last painted. The roof shingles curled with age, and the front lawn was dry with dirt patches. A screen from a lower window rested haphazardly against the building—a tell-tale sign of a makeshift exit.

Thi sat hunched on the front stoop like the weight of the world was upon her shoulders. A half-smoked cigarette dangled between her fingers. She wore a yellow t-shirt, blue shorts, and sandals. When my boots scuffed the sidewalk, Thi looked up and straightened. That movement revealed the Mountain Dew logo on her shirt. A box of cigarettes and a lighter were between her legs.

"You found it," she said.

"I did."

"Gilly said you were coming." Thi motioned to a spot next to her. "Sit down."

"I'm good." I stood in front of her.

She inhaled on her cigarette and shook her head while doing so. When she spoke, light gray smoke escaped her mouth. "I don't like you standing over me, so either I have to stand, or you have to sit. Cut me a break, will you? My sciatica is killing me."

Her English was nearly perfect, and the accent she had was slight.

I sat next to her.

"What do you want to know?" Another inhale on the cigarette. "Same shit as the cops?"

"The cops have contacted you?"

Her face pinched right before she leaned back to rest on her elbows. "Not about Gillian. About my boys."

"Why are the cops looking for your sons?"

She rolled her weight onto her left elbow and waved her right hand. "No, no. That's old news. The cops don't come around anymore. My boys moved out a while ago."

"How many sons do you have?"

"Two."

"Where are they now?"

"One's in Walla Walla, and the other's in the ground."

"I'm sorry."

"Cops." Thi dropped her cigarette to a lower step and crushed it with the heel of her sandal. She spat into the dry grass. "And before you get to worrying that I'm part of anything illegal, that was my boys, not me."

I didn't point out that she was helping an illegal marijuana grower deceive the authorities.

"I kept telling them boys not to get involved with the gangs, but they wouldn't listen. No, don't listen to your mother who knows a thing or two about life."

Thi snatched the box of cigarettes and angrily yanked another one free. She glanced at me and, as an afterthought, offered me the pack. I shook my head. Thi slipped the cigarette between her lips but didn't light it.

"What do you want to know?" she asked. The cigarette bounced as she spoke.

"Have you told anyone about Gillian's operation?"

"Who would I tell?" She motioned around. "This is my life. Just me. I got nobody but Hue and Gilly and that idiot, Eddie."

I studied her.

"Ah, he's fine," she said. She pulled the unlit cigarette from her mouth. "But he looks at us like he can't decide if he wants to do it with one of us or tell us to go back to where we came from."

"I'm sorry."

Thi pointed the filter end of the cigarette at me as if she were going to say something but thought better of it. She lowered her head.

Two semi-trucks drove by, one after the other. Their loud engines overwhelmed every sound in the neighborhood. When they faded into the distance, Thi turned her still-bowed head toward me. "I came to this country as a little girl. Just me and mother. I never met my father."

It was then I noticed the roundness of her eyes, the fullness in her face, and a sprinkling of freckles on her cheeks.

She straightened and looked forward. "The first couple years here, I spent every moment thinking a man in uniform might have been my father." She rolled her eyes. "The first time I saw *M*A*S*H*—you know that show?"

"Yeah," I said. "I watched it last night."

"Reruns." She rolled the unlit cigarette between her thumb and a finger. "I can't stand it anymore, but I watched it as a kid—every Monday night. It gave me this crazy thrill back then. You wouldn't understand. But when I watched that show, I imagined that B.J. Hunnicutt was my father. So stupid. It wasn't even the same war."

"You were a kid," I said.

"I stopped watching when I realized my real father didn't want me any more than he wanted my mother. That's a harsh reality for a child to get used to."

I thought about my daughter. Her mother and I had never married, but I was in Erin's life when I lived in Seattle. When I moved to Spokane, staying involved became harder, but I did my best. Moving away from her was selfish—I knew that now. However, I was running down a destructive path back then. Who knows what I might have done if I didn't leave Seattle? I never wanted to live there again.

Thi continued. "We came here when I was five. Mother raised me to speak English, but more than that, she raised me not to trust anyone. War did that to her. My father did that to her, too." She continued rolling the cigarette between her fingers. "America was supposed to be the land of opportunity. I bet they taught you that in school, and you probably believed it."

I turned a palm upward. What could I say to this woman?

She lit her cigarette. After blowing out a line of smoke, she resumed her story. "We weren't welcomed here. America came to my country to fight a war my mother never understood. Then they left. What was she supposed to do with a soldier's baby? A white man's baby?"

Thi tapped her cigarette even though no ash needed to be knocked free. "The kids in America called me a half-breed." She shrugged. "Not so bad. Better than what they called me back home. A child of the dust—something to be discarded. At least, that's what mother said. I couldn't remember that name." Her gaze took on a faraway look. "Maybe I babied my boys. You know how it is. Trying to make up for how I felt. They got away with too much. I shouldn't have protected them when they did wrong." She inhaled on the cigarette again. "A mother shouldn't do that. She shouldn't pamper her children." Thi glanced at me. "Mother didn't do that for me."

"Did you get in trouble as a kid?"

She shrugged. "Not really. The name-calling bothered me. I tried to hide at home, but mother wouldn't let me. She told me to stand up for myself. To hit the kids who called me names." Her brow furrowed. "But I couldn't do that. I'm not a fighter. I'm too small, and the ones who called me the names were mostly boys." She studied her cigarette again. "I figured out a way to get back at them. I found a boy who *was* a fighter, one who didn't call me names, so I slept with him. He fought for me." She knocked her cigarette, but no ash fell. "I was fourteen."

I let her continue.

"When the first boy got in trouble for fighting, he was sent away. That was too bad because I liked him the most." Thi eyed me. "But I found another one. There was always another one. No one dared call me names anymore. Sometimes, I even pretended they called me names just to hurt some of them. That was a pretty good power until I got pregnant by my fourth protector."

Thi sniffed dismissively and looked away. When she turned back, she said, "Maybe you should be a counselor instead of a detective."

"I haven't said anything."

"You haven't, have you?"

"Where's the father of the boys?"

"Dead. He killed himself when they were still babies. Left me to raise them alone. He couldn't handle the responsibilities of being a man." She studied her cigarette. "You aren't here for this. You want to know if I told anybody about Gilly. Well, I haven't. She pays me to sit and talk with Hue. That's a very good job for a woman with no education."

"How'd you meet Gillian?"

"Through Hue. We're a small community in Spokane."

"The Vietnamese?"

She shook her head. "The children of the dust."

I looked toward the street. A boy and a girl rode by on bicycles. The girl waved at Thi. Both of us returned the gesture. The boy never looked in our direction.

When the kids disappeared down the block, I asked, "Could anybody have followed you?"

"Maybe, but I ride the bus. Same as Hue. I probably would have noticed. And why would anybody care about me? I got nothing anybody would want." Thi thumbed toward herself and then her apartment. "They want some of what I got? They can have at it. They can have it any time they want." Embarrassment flashed over her face. "I didn't mean it like that. I was just—"

I waved off the apology. "I get it."

Her embarrassment vanished and was replaced by intensity. "And what would anyone learn by following me? That I go to a salon most days? Maybe they would think I work there, but we never get customers."

"Has anybody come into the salon while you've been there? Anybody that gives you the heebie-jeebies?"

"Heebie-jeebies?"

"That makes you feel uncomfortable. Have you seen anyone like that?"

She inhaled on the cigarette. "Not inside the store— no."

"Outside?"

"Not really." Thi turned toward me. "But a cop pulled over a car one day. They stopped in our parking lot."

"How long ago was this?"

"Three weeks, maybe."

"What happened?"

"The driver got a ticket. Maybe he was speeding. They do that on Trent."

"No," I said. "What happened with the cop?"

Thi dropped her cigarette to the step and mashed it with the heel of her sandal. "A couple times, I saw him sniffing the air."

"Maybe he smelled the rendering plant."

"Maybe."

"And maybe he smelled the screen-printing shop."

She shrugged.

"What happened after that?"

"The cop went back to his car. It looked like he was writing something."

"Probably the ticket."

"That's what Hue and I thought."

"What kind of cop was he?"

"A white one."

I smiled. "Was he city, county, or a state trooper?"

"He was a white cop. He had a uniform, a gun, and his car had lights. What more does a person like me need to know?"

"Did the cop wear a hat like Smokey Bear? You know him?"

"Only you can prevent forest fires. I remember." Thi shook her head then. "But the cop didn't have a hat like that."

So the cop wasn't a state trooper. "What color was his uniform? Blue or green?"

Blue was the uniform of the Spokane Police Department. Green and tan were the colors of the Spokane County Sheriff's Office.

"Green," Thi said.

"Gillian didn't mention this stop to me."

"I don't think she was there, but I'm sure we told her about it. Maybe she didn't think it was anything. Why? Do you think it might be something?"

I thought about it. There was a county traffic stop in the parking lot of Gillian's building, and the deputy obviously smelled something. Could the driver of the stopped car have sensed it, too? If his window was down, maybe. Probably.

What was the likelihood they smelled marijuana from the building? There was a lot of traffic on Trent Avenue, which meant a variety of smells—the rendering plant, screen-printing chemicals, vehicle exhaust, and who knows what else. The chance of smelling marijuana would be slim.

But if they had, what was the possibility either the deputy or the speeding driver would suspect a grow was in the basement? First, they'd have to know there was a level below the tanning salon and its sister businesses. Second, they would have to correctly assume the smell came from Gillian's building and not from nearby buildings. The chance of them suspecting a grow in the building would be less than slim—it would be razor-thin.

Yet there was still a probability it could have occurred. If the deputy or the driver smelled marijuana and correctly assumed a basement grow in Gillian's building, what were the chances either would mount an illegal raid?

For the cop, I would say it was almost nil. If anything, the deputy would report it and begin surveillance on the building. Once enough evidence was established, his department would write a search warrant and then execute an entry. It would be done in the open, likely with a SWAT team. It wouldn't occur with a concrete block through a window.

But if the driver of the stopped vehicle smelled the grow, what was the likelihood they would mount a raid? It seemed impossibly minuscule. Whoever attempted the attack had some information. The intruders knew about the basement and its entry being inside the tanning salon. The only thing they didn't know about was the security door.

I reminded myself that 'impossibly minuscule' was still possible. I'd have to find out about that traffic stop.

"Can you describe the car that was stopped?"

Thi's eyes rolled upward as she thought. "Red and little."

"That's it?"

"Sporty."

"A little, red, sporty car?"

"Yes."

I stood. "Thank you for your time, Thi."

She rose to her feet and stuck out her hand. Her grip was soft, and her smile pleasing. "I'm sorry for the misunderstanding."

"About?"

Thi motioned toward herself and the apartment. "I'm not a woman that people can help themselves to."

“I understand.”

“Not anymore, at least.” Thi turned and walked up the steps. She never looked back as she entered her apartment. The door quietly closed behind her.

Chapter 9

Police Sergeant Gary Ackerman and I met at Donut Parade, a worn-down coffee shop at the corner of Illinois Avenue and Hamilton Street. He sat at a booth near the back and wore a blue t-shirt, faded jeans, and running shoes. His graying hair, cut in a businessman's style, was slightly tousled.

Overhead, the Beatles' "Penny Lane" softly played through a set of speakers.

I slid into the brown vinyl booth. It moaned and creaked with my movement. A crinkled and folded newspaper sat nearby.

Ackerman had already eaten half of one maple bar. A second waited for him. A ceramic mug of black coffee steamed in his left hand. He eyed my breakfast but didn't comment. I had a cup of black coffee but only a single unglazed cake donut.

"Heading in for your shift?" I asked.

He nodded once.

"What's with the donuts?"

"You got a problem with this place?"

"I figured maybe you'd eat something healthier before starting your day."

Ackerman smirked. "Starting my day. Listen to you." He held up his donut. "I can't do this in uniform. You know how it is, so I didn't think you'd mind when you said pick the place. But now you're sounding like my wife. Did she hire you to keep an eye on me? Is that what this is?"

I smiled. "No."

"Because this is as racy as my life gets. Sneaking donuts once a week." He shook his head ruefully. "She wants me to live a long time, so it's no refined sugars or wheat in our house." He bit into the donut. He murmured his appreciation of the taste before asking, "Is a long life even worth it without donuts?"

"How's the promotion?"

Until recently, Ackerman had been a Major Crimes detective. We met when he investigated the murder of a friend of mine. He took an interest in me due to my former life as a Seattle cop. He was a decent guy who deeply loved his wife. He had a son who died before we'd ever met.

I wasn't surprised when he told me he'd been promoted to sergeant earlier in the year. Even though Major Crimes was the pinnacle of the investigative world, Ackerman seemed to be a man on a mission. Whenever we talked about things bigger than the moment, topics like goals and legacy would arise.

He shrugged. "Going back to graveyard is harder than expected, but I'll get used to it. Are we going to dance around much longer, or are you going to tell me why we're here?"

"Can't we get together like friends?"

"Sure," he said, "but this isn't that."

"How do you know?"

Ackerman studied me, and I sipped my coffee.

"Friends do things regularly, John. You only call when you need something."

"You've called when you've needed help, too." It sounded defensive and whiny—like an emotionally wounded high-school girlfriend. I wished I had said something different or, better yet, kept my mouth shut.

The stuff Ackerman asked me to help with wasn't illegal, but they were things I specifically could assist with. He knew I had connections to people like Deacon Hogue and Gary Gaspar. A couple of times, I poked around the fringes of the criminal underworld and provided him some intel that helped build a case. He kept my name out of the report, and he looked so much smarter for it.

Ackerman took another bite and then dropped his donut onto a napkin. He waited to speak until he finished. "That's the point. We call each other when we need things. We don't get together for a Mariners game. We never meet for beers on a Friday night. And we haven't once helped the other with a home project. So, let's stop pretending that we're friends and get down to business."

"No."

He cocked his head.

"I'm sorry, Gary."

"Don't give me that."

"For real." I briefly looked away. When I faced him again, I leaned in. "I am sorry. I've considered you a friend, but I haven't treated you that way. You're a good guy—"

"C'mon," he interrupted.

"—and I tend to take that for granted in people. Forget why I called. Let's just eat our donuts and act like a couple regular dudes."

"Dudes?"

"You know what I mean." I broke my first donut in half and dipped it into my coffee. "How are the Mariners doing?"

"Bite me." Ackerman rarely, if ever, swore. "You know exactly how they're doing, so dispense with the pleasantries."

I shoved the soaked donut section into my mouth. After swallowing, I said, "I'll get what I want some other way. I'm serious. You made a good point." I lifted my chin toward his donuts. "I didn't know you liked maple bars."

"You're pissing me off, John."

I interlaced my fingers and rested my forearms against the table's edge. "Are you sure?"

"I'm gonna reach across this table and smack you in the mouth."

"Okay," I said, "but only because you asked so nicely."

He scowled.

"I'd like to know about a county traffic stop."

Ackerman's scowl relaxed, but a frown remained. "Put in a records request."

"I can't."

"Why not?"

"Because I don't have enough information about it. I know a deputy stopped a car at a certain location and a general date, but that's it."

"I can search for it by that." He sipped his coffee. "What do you want to know when I find it?"

"What was the disposition of the stop?"

"That's it?"

I nodded.

"Why's that matter?"

My gaze drifted over the other customers. No one seemed to be listening to us, so I returned my attention to Ackerman. "I don't know if it does matter, but I'm trying to ask for your help without causing you to violate your department's protocols."

Ackerman slipped the final bit of donut into his mouth.

I continued. "I figure if you tell me the disposition, that'll let me know enough." It wouldn't, but I needed to get my foot in the door with the sergeant. I needed him to say yes to something before I could weasel some further information from him. It wasn't very friendly to think that, but I didn't know any other way to get this information.

He asked, "Where did this stop happen?"

I gave him the address of Gillian's building.

"That's in the county."

"But you can still see who made the stop, right? And what the disposition of it was?"

Ackerman slid his second donut in front of him. "What's at this location?"

"Nothing important. Just a small retail building, but it's the parking lot that matters. It's where the two vehicles stopped."

"Why's this traffic stop important?"

Ackerman was smart. The guy wouldn't bite on a line of bullshit. I would have preferred the truth—that was always the simplest and easiest to remember, especially if he asked questions about it in the future. Therefore, evasion seemed better than an outright lie.

I said, "I can't explain it right now."

"You're asking me to trust you?"

"I am."

"You're not rooting around in any of our cases, are you? Or any of the county's cases? That didn't turn out so good when you did it with us."

"I remember, and I'm not doing that. I promise."

Ackerman ripped a corner off the second maple bar. He pointed it at me. "And you only want to know the disposition of that stop?"

"That's right," I lied.

He popped the small bite of donut into his mouth. He removed a pen from his pocket and pulled a napkin toward him. His thumb clicked the tip of the pen out. "What's that address again?"

I told him.

"What day did it happen?"

"I don't know exactly, but about two, maybe three, weeks ago."

He lifted his eyebrows, but he didn't look up. "What kind of car?"

"A little, red sporty one."

Now he raised his eyes. "That's all I get?"

"Besides, it was a county officer, that's all I've got to give."

Ackerman rolled his eyes. "It's a good thing we're such close friends."

"I already said I was sorry."

When Ackerman finished writing, he clicked the top of the pen, and the tip disappeared. "It's not a lot to work with, but I'll give it a shot. And I'm telling you, this better not be anything more than a traffic infraction. If it is, we're going to have more words."

"I understand." I dipped the other half of the donut into my coffee. "So, what should we talk about next? The Seahawks? How do you think they're going to do this year?"

Ackerman smirked. "Don't start."

***

My cell phone rang. "Cutler," I said.

"It's Remo. You wanna talk?"

"Where are you?" He sounded funny, but there was loud traffic noise and what sounded like a jackhammer in the background.

"On my way to The Well," Remo said. "Ever been?"

"Yeah."

"Meet me there."

I wanted to meet someplace quiet, but he hung up before I could protest. I needed info from him, though. Better for him to be comfortable and happy.

It took a few minutes to get downtown. I couldn't find a spot along the curb, so I left my truck in a neighboring Diamond Parking lot. For a moment, I thought about paying the hourly rate but decided the likelihood of any checker stumbling across my vehicle was slim. I'd skirted paying for parking before. It never felt like that big of a deal to me. If I ever got a fine, I'd still be dollars ahead.

Inside The Well, Elva Lightly stood behind the bar. She lifted her chin in acknowledgment, then jerked her head toward a darkened corner.

On the radio, a singer said, "Something's happening here." It was a hippie mainstay and one I sort of liked. I didn't know the band or the name of the tune. However, it seemed an out-of-place sentiment for The Well.

At the bar, two drunks sat slumped over their cans of Pabst. Several chairs separated them.

Only two tables were occupied.

A mixed couple sat at the first. Several empty glasses had accumulated on the table. He was an elderly white man—too fat, bald, and pale for the young black woman seated next to him. She might have been a model had life on the streets not scuffed her like an old tennis shoe. He wore a suit and a tie. She wore a skirt and a t-shirt. He watched her with watery eyes as she lazily sipped her drink through a straw. It wasn't hard to figure out that relationship.

Only a single man sat at the other table—Remo. Using both hands, he crushed his empty can of Pabst. "You found me."

I sat across from him. "You weren't that hard to find."

He chuckled. "I've been trying to find myself for years."

I leaned in. We were in a darkened corner, so getting a decent look at his pupils was difficult. My eyes hadn't adjusted to the low light of the bar yet. Even if they had, I'm not sure I could see the tell-tale signs.

Remo pulled back into the shadow. "This is my sister's joint." His words slurred together. "What do ya think? Pretty great, huh?"

I nodded.

"Ever been?"

"Elva and I go way back."

Remo looked toward his sister. "Is that so? I didn't know that." His attention returned to me. "That's cool, man. I'm glad. Like really. How're things going with Gilly?"

"That's what I wanted to talk about."

Elva arrived at our table and plopped two cans of Pabst down.

"Hey," Remo said. He carelessly waved his hand between us. "I didn't know you guys knew each other."

Elva snapped the first one open. "Oh, yeah. This guy and me got history."

"That's what he said. You guys hook up or something?"

She set the can in front of her brother but didn't let go. "Maybe you should lay off, Remo."

He seemed offended by her accusation. "I'm not hurting no one."

"That's your last one."

"But I just got here."

"You've been drinking elsewhere."

He smirked. "What kind of sister are you?"

"The kind who looks out for you." Elva let go of his beer and eyed me. She grabbed the second can, but I waved her off.

"No, thanks," I said. "I'm not drinking."

She snapped open the can anyway and thunked it on the table. Beer foamed up from the hole. "Six bucks. He got started 'fore you came in."

Remo grabbed his beer and took a healthy swallow. When he lowered the can, his gaze drifted elsewhere in the bar.

I pulled out my wallet and handed Elva a ten. She lifted it in a show of appreciation.

"For my tip."

The song on the radio changed. It was some disco thing I tried to ignore, but the couple at the table behind us laughed.

"Oh, yeah," the old man said. His voice was low and heavy with alcohol.

There was a sound of chairs sliding back, and I looked over my shoulder. The couple got up to dance. The older man's feet stayed rooted to the floor as he swayed. The younger woman held her drink to her chest as she slowly backed into him. Her hips moved in rhythm with the music. Her eyes stayed closed, and she sipped her drink. Maybe I'd been wrong. Perhaps it was love.

"You going to drink that?"

I turned back to find Remo pointing at my beer. I pushed the can toward the middle of the table. He grabbed it and pulled it the rest of the way to him. He clutched both cans as if they were the arms of a life preserver.

He leaned slightly to watch our neighbors. Even though the disco song continued to play, the couple stopped dancing and laughed with exhausted pleasure. The older man fell heavily into his chair as his younger date gently settled in. He waved at Elva for another round.

"What's wrong, Remo? I didn't know you to be much of a drinker."

"So, Gilly?" he said, ignoring my question. "What do you want to know?"

"Who's your supplier?"

"Gilly. You know—"

"The former one."

Remo's brow furrowed.

"Don't think it over," I said. "Just tell me the guy's name."

He sipped from the first beer. "Why do you need that?"

"Because I want to talk with him."

"But why for?"

"I'm wondering what he did after you told him you quit."

Remo's face pinched. "Aw, shit, man. Don't talk to him." He sipped from the second beer now. "I told him I was doing the real estate. You know, the shit everybody's doing now."

"How drunk are you?"

He waved a beer. "It looks so easy. Slap some paint on the walls. Drop in some new carpet. Big money. No whammies." He clicked the two cans of beer together. "So much safer than selling chronic to lawyers and teachers."

"Is that what you told him?"

"Why not? I don't look like I can swing a hammer?"

"You told me you couldn't."

He appeared confused. "I did? When?"

"Back at your place."

"Oh." He exaggeratedly shook his head and then sipped from the first beer. "But you're stirring up dead horses with this." Another sip, but from the second beer this time. He refused to make eye contact with me now.

"What's going on, Remo?"

"Nothing. I swear."

I leaned in. "Bullshit, it's nothing. You're double fisting it like the world is about to end."

"Maybe it is." He kicked back the first can and drained it. "Maybe it is," he muttered.

"What happened?"

Remo again bent to the side to check out the couple. They were canoodling now. When he eyed me again, he whispered, "Double G happened. He came and saw me."

"When?"

"This morning."

I wondered if Gaspar's visit was before or after I saw him. Probably after when I had stirred him up about the rumor. Either he was searching for what I knew, or he already knew about Gillian's enterprise and wanted to confirm how I was involved.

"What'd he want?" I asked.

"To talk. Least that's what he said, but you never know with Double G. Guy tells you a lie with the left hand then hits you with truth in his right. When has Double G ever stopped by to chit-chat with anybody?"

His question sounded awfully close to Gary Ackerman's admonishment of me. I didn't like being lumped in with Double G's behavior. I needed to be better than that. Remo tipped back the second can and drank the remaining beer in one long swallow.

"What specifically did Double G ask you, Remo?"

His eyes widened with fear. "You, man. Well, and me, too, I guess. He knew you and I were at my house. Somebody saw us there. How'd they do that?"

"What'd you tell him?"

"Nothing," Remo hissed. "I told him nothing! I'm not a rat!"

"Hey!" the old man said from behind me. "Keep it down over there."

"Keep down yerself," Remo said. Then he added under his breath, "You ol' whoremonger."

"Where did Double G find you?" I asked.

Remo twisted the empty can until it crumpled in his hands. "Outside my apartment. It was like they were waiting for me or something. Shit, I'm gonna have to move now."

"Did Double G make it sound like he knew about Gillian's grow?"

He shook his head. "Nuh-uh. I don't think he knew nothing about it. He asked what you and I were conspiring to do. That's how he said it, too. *Conspiring.* Like we're about to overthrow the government. Geez, that guy gives me the creeps."

"He didn't give you the creeps before?"

Remo's eyes narrowed. "That was before I screwed up. Now, I'm not so keen on him. You shouldn't be so keen on him either as he seemed real interested in you. Like maybe he has a crush on you or something."

"And what did you tell him?"

"Nothing. I swear to Christ, man." He grabbed the second beer can and crushed it. "Like I'll promise on the bible and say amen and do all that fancy Catholic jazz." He crossed his right hand horizontally across his chest. Beer dribbled from the compressed can, leaving a thin trail over his shirt.

I rubbed my face. Had my mentioning an attempted heist of a county marijuana grow created that much interest in Double G? Or was he involved from the jump? The more I thought about it, the more convinced I became that I sent Double G on that hunt. He went to Remo to pump information.

"What about your previous dealer?"

He rolled his eyes. "Not this again."

"You thought I forgot."

"I mighta hoped."

"Well, I didn't. I want to know who you left for Gillian."

His expression seemed pained. "Why's it matter?"

"Maybe that guy did something stupid. Maybe that guy got jealous that you left him for someone else."

Remo's eyes brightened. "You think so?"

"I don't know, but maybe."

"I would never have thought." He tossed the crushed can in the air and caught it. "I mean, I got a pretty good reputation, so I could see that happening."

"The name."

Remo tossed the can and caught it once more. "Trevor Kobold."

"And he thinks you're selling real estate?"

"That's right."

"Are you sure you convinced him?"

Remo set the crumbled can onto the table. "I think so." I stared at him.

"What? I do. I don't know if he believed it for sure, but I think so."

Remo lifted his hand for another beer, but Elva called out, "You've had enough."

"Aw, c'mon, Elva!"

"I'll bring you some water, and then you can have another."

Remo eyed me. He whispered, "Will you drink it?"

"Sure. What happened with your book of business?"

"Huh?"

"Your clients, Remo."

He smirked. "Ah, like an insurance salesman, you mean."

"Twenty years is a lot of clients."

"You wouldn't believe." He thumped himself in the chest. "If I worked for a company, they woulda given me a gold watch or something. Maybe even a company car."

"What happened to your clients when you left Trevor?"

"I was supposed to give my clients the number of the new guy, the guy they'd buy from instead of me."

"And did you?"

"Some. Just the jerks I wanted to dump." He proudly thumped himself again. "I'm not stupid."

"Of course not."

He shot me a sideways glance. "Hey! I couldn't give them all up. I needed to keep the good ones for myself."

"Trevor had to know that only a few of your clients called."

"Maybe. How would I know?"

Elva walked over and set a glass of water in front of Remo. "Drink that."

"I will."

She angrily pointed at it. "Do it while I'm standing here. I don't trust you not to pass it to this guy as soon as I walk away."

Remo rolled his eyes. "You can trust me, Elva. I'm your brother."

She crossed her arms.

Reluctantly, he picked up the glass and drank it. Tendrils of water ran down the sides of his mouth.

Overhead, another disco song started. I had no idea what it was called or who performed it, but the older man seemed excited to hear it. "Another good one," he said. The couple remained seated, though.

When Remo finished with the water, he handed Elva the glass.

"Was that so hard?" she asked.

"Now, can I have another? And bring him one, too."

I said, "No," but Elva was already walking back to the bar.

Remo watched her walk away. "You sure you know my sister? You don't seem her type."

"About Trevor. He never tried to call and find out what's up with the lack of clients?"

"He might have called."

"Might have?"

Remo appeared sheepish. "I don't know. I got rid of that number after I left him. I called all my people and told them I got a new phone."

"Sort of like what you did to me."

"Hey, man." Remo shook his head. "How many times have I got to apologize for that?"

"Once would be a nice start."

"Fine. Geez. Whatever."

Elva headed back our way. She held two cans. "I'm not even going to pretend." She set both on the table and then held out her hand. "Ten bucks."

I dug out another bill and gave it to her. She slipped it from my fingers. "That's your last one, Remo."

He grabbed both beers and pulled them to him.

"Your last two," she corrected. She clucked her tongue and walked away.

"What's Trevor look like?" I asked.

"He looks like Trevor. What am I supposed to say?" Remo snapped open a can and tilted it back.

"What color is he?"

Remo wiped the back of his hand over his wet lips. "That's a racist question."

"I've been nice so far, Remo, but I can always bust you in the teeth."

"With Elva over there?"

"She said it was okay as long as I didn't do it inside the apartment."

Remo's face flattened. "He's white."

"How old is he?"

"I never saw his driver's license."

I balled a fist for him to see. "Take a guess."

"Thirty-five." He scooted his chair back from the table and took both beers with him. "But I could be wrong."

"Mid-thirties?"

"What do I know?"

"Where can I find Trevor?"

Remo sipped from the opened beer. "Last I knew, he lived at a place on Division. Over near the General Store. You know the place?"

"I'm gonna need a little more than that."

"It's not like we send each other Christmas cards. It's a blue house on the east side—" His eyes rolled toward the ceiling. The beer cans danced back and forth as he thought. "No. The west side. Definitely, the west side. He's in a blue house near the General Store."

"It's on Division. Not a side street? Because I'm trying to place some houses there, and all I'm envisioning are businesses."

Remo appeared slightly embarrassed. "Behind those businesses."

"Why don't you show me where?"

He clutched the beers to his chest. "I don't want to see Trevor. He'll know I lied to him. You can find it. Trust me. It's a blue house on one of those side streets away from the General Store. Like, how many blue houses could there be?"

"Give me something else. A blue house is not enough."

"Shit, Cutler. I don't know."

I stood, stepped around the table, and grabbed his shirt. "Either give me something, or you're going with me."

"He likes gnomes!"

"Leave the boy alone," the old man said.

"Not in here!" Elva hollered. "Take it outside."

I released Remo's shirt. "Gnomes?"

"Yeah," he said. "Trevor collects them. They totally freak me out. Like a bunch of little Double G's or something. Just staring at me all the damn time."

***

I returned home for a late lunch. The donut and coffee I had earlier weren't cutting it.

It was getting deep into the afternoon, so maybe I should have skipped eating and waited to grab an early dinner. Or perhaps I might have ordered something small at a fast-food joint so I could have continued working. The reality was I wanted a short break to go home. That's the benefit of working for oneself.

I made lunch and joined the dog in the backyard. He hid in the shade while I sat on the steps with a ham and cheddar sandwich and a side of chips.

A car pulled up out front—both the dog and I heard its engine. Corporal cocked his head. At this time of day, the car might have been someone visiting the park or the nearby community center. It wasn't worth getting too excited about.

Someone knocked at the front of the house.

"Here you go," I said and held out the remaining sandwich to Corporal. He trotted over and snatched it from my fingers. His tail wagged as it disappeared in a single bite.

The knocking persisted.

I left the dog outside and entered the house. It was a quick walk through the kitchen into the living room. Due to the day's heat, both doors to the house were open, and a large fan spun the air about.

She and I made eye contact through the screen door.

Tanya Robertson didn't wait for an invitation. She pulled the door open and stepped inside. It was the first time I'd seen her since she walked out of my apartment a couple of years ago. She wore a white top, black shorts, and black high heels. Her skin was deeply tanned, and a pair of sunglasses were pushed on top of her head. As always, she looked fantastic.

There was something in her eyes—a look I'd seen before. She'd been drinking. I shouldn't judge. I'd been day drinking on Sunday, but this was almost four on a Tuesday—a workday for most folks. But Tanya never worked—a luxury provided through marriage and a subsequent divorce settlement.

"This is where you live now," she said. Tanya's eyes flicked to the desk and its computer. Paperwork was haphazardly spread about. "And work, too, I guess." Tanya's gaze flitted around the room. It seemed she carefully indexed everything she saw. "You should hire a decorator."

The former version of myself might have found that statement an opportunity to flirt with her—to ask if she'd want to help. But Tanya wasn't a woman I wanted back in my life for many reasons.

My relationship with Stacy was the immediate excuse, but I hadn't forgotten how I felt about Tanya. Love is a balancing act—a constant game of teeter-totter. Neither participant should get too far out on one side, or the whole thing would be out of whack. With Tanya, we started the seesaw in the middle—we were happy not to care about the other. Eventually, I developed feelings that left me on the far end. She never left the middle.

"Why are you here?" I asked.

"After all this time, that's the greeting I get?" She shimmied her shoulders a little. "I thought maybe you missed me. You know, be happy to see me. That sort of thing."

I stared at her.

"Don't I look good?"

She did. Damn good. But that was never the problem with Tanya.

I said, "You look drunk."

Her face flattened. "One drink. Gimme a break."

"Fine."

She waved my comment away. "Maybe two, but that's it. What of it?"

I spread my hands to show my indifference.

"You didn't use to be such a stick in the mud."

That slight wouldn't get a rise out of me.

"It's her that's doing it to you. She's a goddamned fun-sponge." Her face hardened. "Why are you doing this?"

"Doing what?"

"You know what you're doing." She stepped forward and waggled a finger between the two of us. "This."

I moved away from Tanya. "I'm not doing anything."

"Bullshit!" Her voice rose. "You're doing it to get even." She tapped her chest. "You're both doing it!"

I kept my voice calm. "There's nothing to get even about."

Her fists balled, and she leaned into me. Spittle was on her lips. "Why did you break up with me? Huh? Why?"

"We never had anything."

She threw her arms into the air. "Yes, we did." Tanya turned in a circle and then reached out but stopped short of touching my face. She pulled back and lightly touched her own. "We had something special."

"You didn't think it was special at the time."

Tanya pulled her arms tight to her body. "Yes, I did. Yes, I *did*. You know I did."

I shook my head. "You only care because of Stacy."

"That's not true. It's not." Tanya dropped her arms and thrust her chin out. "She's not better than me. You know that, right? Little sister is nothing but a cheap copy."

I motioned toward the door. "You should go."

"Wait." She held up her hands. "I'm sorry."

"Tanya," I said.

"How'd you two even meet?"

I didn't answer.

Her eyes flicked to my computer. "You probably looked her up." Tanya's face soured. "Mr. Detective found my sister. That's what you did. Then you revenge fucked her."

I pointed over her shoulder. "It's time you go."

"I'm right!" She grabbed her head. "That's why you did it." She hit me in the arm. "Tell me I'm right!"

"Go."

She hit me several times, but they were largely symbolic slaps across the upper arms and one slap across the chest. No strike ever hit my face. I'm not sure I would have stopped her had she struck me there.

Tanya quickly tired herself out and leaned her head against my chest. I grabbed her by her upper arms. There was no way I would hug her or hold her. I would never tell her things would be all right.

"You need to go," I said flatly.

She looked up. "Why do you hate me?"

"It's time to leave."

Tears welled in her eyes. It was a big dramatic cry that was mostly for my benefit. "Didn't I make you happy?"

"We weren't that type of thing."

Tanya reached for me, but I pushed her away. She staggered backward before she caught her balance.

"You liked what we were!" She pointed at me. "You loved me, John Cutler. I know you did."

"Do you need a cab?"

She stiffened, and her lip curled. "I'm fine. I can drive my fucking self." Tanya walked to the door but stopped before stepping out. She looked back and glowered at me. "Seems we're making a habit of this." She flipped me off.

The screen door closed behind her.

***

Across from the General Store, on the west side of Division Street, were several businesses. There was an auto repair joint, a car rental business, and a home decor company.

There were also three side streets—York Avenue, Carlisle Avenue, and Jackson Avenue. To satisfy my curiosity, I counted blue homes in the area. There were seven in a block-and-a-half radius of those three streets.

But only one home on York Avenue had a menagerie of colorful gnomes guarding its entrance. An older Honda Passport sat curbside in front of a Craftsman-style house that I suspected belonged to Trevor Kobold.

I circled the block once before parking down the way. Before getting out, I pulled my gun from the glove box. Approaching a drug dealer unarmed didn't feel like the smartest choice. I tucked the gun into the back of my pants and pulled my shirt down over it.

Then I took my time walking to Kobold's home. I proceeded to the blue house through the phalanx of clay and plastic gnomes. The pale, chubby faces were abnormally pleasant, and many of the characters were posed in ridiculous manners. One stood on his hands.

Another waved at me. Yet another stared at me through a pair of binoculars.

I didn't usually hate gnomes but seeing so many at once creeped me out. Maybe that was their job—to make visitors uncomfortable.

The property wasn't well-maintained. The lawn needed both watering and mowing. Shingles from the roof lay in the landscaping bark. Paint chipped off the side of the clapboard siding.

I knocked on the front door and waited.

Eventually, a door opened, and a white man in his late twenties looked dreamily at me as if he might have just woken up. He wore only basketball shorts, and a tattoo of a marijuana leaf adorned his hairless chest. He pushed an errant strand of blond hair from his face. "Yeah?"

"Is Trevor in?"

"And you are?"

"John Cutler."

The guy absently scratched his chest. "Doesn't ring a bell."

"It shouldn't. Is Trevor home?"

"Nuh-uh." Now, his eyes focused, and his head tilted slightly. "What's this about?"

"I'll stop by later."

I turned to leave.

"Hey."

I stopped and glanced over my shoulder.

"You a cop or something?"

"No."

"Then what's this about?"

"I'll come back later."

His eyes narrowed. "Whatever." He shut the door.

Chapter 10

The dog and I were on a walk near the Spokane River. We'd just walked down Pettet Drive, known around town as Doomsday Hill. Supposedly, it wiped out many runners of the Bloomsday race. I'd never attended that event nor attempted to run the hill away from the competition. I did, however, walk it frequently with the dog. That alone was a decent challenge.

Corporal was off-leash and roamed the trail ahead of me. My cell phone buzzed, and I pulled it from my pocket. I expected a call from her, but I thought it would have come sooner.

Without introduction, Stacy Mathers said, "Tanya stopped by again. Blasted out of her mind."

"I figured."

"Wait." There were a couple of beats before she asked, "Did she go over to your place?"

"Yeah."

"Oh." I could hear an entire history of sisterly insecurities in that single word. "She didn't say."

"Nothing happened."

"Okay."

"I promise, Stacy. Listen, she came over. She'd had too much to drink."

Stacy clucked. "You said she wouldn't show up drunk."

"I was wrong, but it didn't matter. She got upset. Cried a little. We had some back and forth before I sent her on her way."

"Back and forth." Her words were careful and respectful. "What's that mean? You don't have to tell me if you don't want."

"It means she wanted to talk, and I wasn't having any of it."

Several beats of silence passed before Stacy asked, "Why not?"

"You know why."

Now, there was a longer pause. I stopped walking and covered my open ear with a hand.

"Are you still there?" I asked.

Stacy sighed. "She wants me to break it off with you, John. She threatened we wouldn't be sisters anymore."

Now, it was my turn for the silence.

"Can you come over?" she asked.

"Three nights in a row is dangerously close to a thing."

"Shut up, John."

She sounded worried, and I made a joke in avoidance. Classic Cutler, I thought. "Yeah, hey, I'm sorry. What time?"

"When you can, but don't worry. The door will be unlocked. Be quiet when you come in. I'll get the kids to bed early."

"I can come now, but I'm on a walk with the dog and—"

"Take your time. I still need to wrap my head around all this."

The call ended.

***

I'd like to say that I took my time walking Corporal and that I didn't hustle back up Doomsday Hill. I'd also like to say that I didn't race through a shower and didn't drive a little too quickly to Stacy's house.

But that didn't happen.

It wasn't like it was my first time seeing her. The thrill of new passion faded some time ago. There was still some odd excitement to sneaking into her house. That part never left. Yet that wasn't why I hurried.

I rushed because Stacy was upset, and I feared I might lose her.

Our relationship wasn't an all-encompassing infatuation that I'd had with a woman in Seattle. I thought that was love, but it was a destructive connection. My resulting behavior cost me a job and my self-respect. Then I met a woman while working at Club Royale. I loved her but put helping an old friend over her feelings. She wouldn't let that go, and, in retrospect, I couldn't blame her.

Even though I liked Stacy, we weren't exclusive. I was open to our relationship being more, but she kept me at bay because of her kids. Due to our dynamic, there'd been a couple of other women in the time we'd known each other. If Stacy and I weren't anything more than convenient, then I wasn't going to sit on the sidelines. Those other lovers were like Stacy and me—simply convenient.

So, if my recent romantic life was built around the concept of convenience, then why was I running over to a woman's house on a late summer evening to ease her feelings? That didn't feel so convenient.

As promised, Stacy's front door was unlocked. I entered quietly, walked up the stairs, down the hallway, and into her bedroom. There was an odd expectation that Stacy would be naked. Or in a nightie. Maybe wrapped only in a towel. She often removed as many barriers as possible.

But Stacy sat cross-legged in the middle of her bed. She wore jeans and a t-shirt. Her face was calm, and she seemed almost serene. A noise machine on the nightstand played the sound of a babbling brook.

"Shut the door," she whispered. After doing so, I faced her. She patted the bed. "Can we talk?"

My heart raced as I feared what she was about to say. "Listen—"

She patted the bed again. "Please sit, John."

I sat on the bed but not next to her. My back rested against the headboard. It wouldn't be the first time a woman ended a relationship with me. I did my best to appear stoic and detached.

"I like you," she said.

That wasn't what I had expected, but it was in line with breakup patter. My smile felt crooked, maybe condescending, but I didn't bother to correct it. If she wanted to end what we had, I wouldn't grovel. She could play her cards, then I'd walk out of that house with my head held high.

Stacy said, "This thing with Tanya has got me thinking."

I crossed my arms. Here it comes, I thought.

"We didn't get into this for the wrong reasons, did we?"

"Not me."

She averted her eyes and lowered her head. "When I called you—the first time, I mean—I said I wanted to talk. You know, to get a man's opinion."

"I remember."

Stacy's head remained bowed. "I didn't care what you thought about my divorce or anyone for that matter. I called you because I knew what you and Tanya had."

I didn't answer. I knew that's why she called, but I never called bullshit on her story. I let her have the lie—I let *us* have it.

She looked up, and remorse filled her eyes. We sat silently for several minutes and listened to the sound machine produce its digital babbling brook.

Stacy had grown up in the shadow of her sister, the model. Tanya had been a runner-up for Miss Teen Washington. Stacy was an attractive woman in her own right, but a sister keen on running for titles creates certain competitions in a family. That led to Stacy overcompensating with her studies. She achieved in areas that Tanya was weak, but that hadn't made her happy.

She rubbed her hands together. "I'm glad she found out, John. It was bound to happen sooner or later."

"Sure."

Her eyes narrowed. "I told her everything today. Do you want to know why?"

I waited for her to hurry up and break it off with me. I didn't need all the reasons that brought her to this moment. "Not really."

Stacy looked away. "Why'd you start with me?"

"Are you kidding?"

She looked at me again, and now hurt was in her eyes. She wanted an answer, and I avoided it with a joke. Christ, what was I doing? "You were pretty, and you seemed nice."

That seemed to make her happy, and I was glad because it was the truth.

Stacy's brow furrowed as she inhaled deeply. "I like you, John. I like you a lot. And I'm okay with Tanya being mad at me because of it."

Maybe she wasn't going to break up with me.

"But I'm not willing to lose a sister with the way our situation is."

Then again, perhaps I was wrong.

Stacy nervously rubbed her hands some more. "What I'm saying is this—if you want to keep this relationship on the down-low, then I think we should end it."

"The down-low was your idea. For the kids, remember?"

She nodded. "But that needs to change if you and I are to have anything long-term."

"What are you saying?"

"I want us to be something more."

I cocked my head.

"I want you to meet my kids, for you to come over for dinners. I want us to do things out in the open where people can see us. You know, go out like a real couple. I'll get a babysitter."

"Maybe you could ask Tanya."

Her eyes widened. "Oh, I don't think so, but that's what I want. If you want to be with me, that's where this has to go. But if that's not something you want, then I'll understand."

I scooted next to her. "Let's do it."

"Not so fast." She slipped off the bed. "You need to take a night and think about this. There are kids involved."

"I know. I have a daughter."

"No offense, John, but she's a teenager who lives on the other side of the state." She pointed off in the distance. "These kids here are going to want to talk with you, play with you, be around you. I'm not asking for you to be their father, they've already got one, but if you're in their lives, you're in their lives for real. Do you get what I'm saying?"

I stood in front of her. "I understand. This is what I want."

Stacy touched the side of my face. "Go home and think about this."

"I don't need to."

"For me. *Please*." She grabbed me by the neck, pulled me down, and kissed my forehead. "Take it seriously."

I nodded several times before padding out of her house.

***

An irritating, persistent buzzing awoke me from a dreamless sleep. I rolled over and reached for my cell phone. The red letters on the alarm clock were blurry. I blinked, and they came into focus. It was a few minutes after three.

Calls at that time of day were never good. I half-expected the call to be from Stacy. She never phoned this late for me to come over, but after our earlier conversation, maybe she had some late-night reservations.

It wasn't her.

I opened the phone. "Cutler."

"There's been a shooting," Gillian Brewer said. Before I could ask who and where, she continued. "Rock got shot."

"Is he okay?"

"Yeah. He got one of the intruders."

I sat upright, and Corporal moved to the bedside. "Are the cops there?"

"No. Oh God, John. It's a mess. They busted the window again."

"What are you doing about Rock?"

"The Souls have some doctor. They already took him there. Can you come and help?"

I stared at the ceiling.

"John?" The fear in her voice was unmistakable. "You don't owe me anything, but I could use someone in my corner right now."

"I'll be there in a few."

***

I arrived at Gillian's building a little more than thirty minutes later. I expected to see motorcycles and vehicles in front of the building, but the lot was empty. However, there was activity.

Three men in leather vests and blue jeans were in front of Sunshine Smiles. Two held the large piece of plywood while the third drilled screws into it. On the back of their vests were several patches. A rocker on the top read *Wasted Souls*. The lower rocker read *Spokane, WA*. In the middle of the vests was the club's logo—a grinning skull shrouded in rising smoke.

The sidewalk in front of the tanning salon appeared wet.

When I pulled into the parking lot, the headlights of my truck swept over the three men. One of the guys holding the plywood turned toward me and repeatedly dragged his hand over his throat. His angry look made it clear he wasn't happy about being illuminated. I clicked off the headlights and pulled into a parking spot at the front of the building.

The same guy who'd gestured at me to turn off my lights now thumbed for me to move my truck. He motioned toward the end of the building. The other guy holding the plywood frowned. Even the guy with the drill stopped to eye me.

How many bikers did it take to tell me I screwed up? Three, it seemed.

I backed out of the parking spot and crept the truck around the edge of the building. My headlights remained off. Once in the back, I found Gillian's Audi and four motorcycles. Gravel crunched under my tires as the truck moved slowly forward.

After slipping the gearshift into Park, I reached for my glove box. Before I could get the gun out, a man a few years older than me exited from the rear of the tanning salon. He studied me with open curiosity. I left the gun where it was and got out.

The man wore the same get-up that the guys in the front did. He had long dark hair and several days of growth on his face. He had a softening midsection, but his scowl showed him a man not to be tested. "Cutler?"

I nodded.

"Booster," he said.

We didn't shake hands.

He motioned with his head toward the building. "She's inside." Booster held up a hand to stop me from entering. "Hold on."

I waited.

"Don't give me the stink eye, pal. We're on the same side here."

"Didn't know I was doing that," I said.

"These jagoffs don't know who they're fucking with."

"I'm sure."

"You get any idea of who these hitters are, you tell me." Booster pounded his chest with the top of his fist. "We'll make that problem go away. *Permanently*."

I stared at him.

"Gilly is family."

"I didn't know a sister-in-law qualified for club status."

Booster's face flattened. "Don't be a smart ass, Cutler. We don't know each other."

I raised my hands in deference. "Trying to understand the rules."

"They were just explained to you."

"Can I go and see my client?"

Booster stepped out of the way and motioned me inside. "Can't wait to see a real-life detective in action."

Gillian sat with her head down in the darkness of the lobby. She wore a long-sleeved red shirt, white pants, and red shoes. Even at this time of night, the woman looked put together.

The ambient light from the parking lot provided enough illumination to see. Blood was in the middle of the floor—not a lot but enough. Another cinder block lay near Gillian's feet.

She looked up when I entered the room. Booster followed me, but he soon stopped and leaned against the hallway wall.

"You see what they did?" Gillian pointed at the blood, then the window. "As soon as we replaced the glass, they attacked again. Rock…" She lowered her head.

"How is he?"

From behind me, Booster said, "He'll live. Took one in the shoulder." He reached out and tapped the wall where a bullet had entered. "They sprayed a few rounds. There's another over there. I've already dug out the slugs." He reached into a pocket and pulled out two small chunks of metal. I couldn't tell what caliber they were. "Rock is damn lucky he didn't get hit with all three. We've got him with our doctor now."

"What about the other guy?" I asked.

"They dragged him off," Booster said. "He's either dead, or he's in a bad way. Rock hit him with the persuader. Gut shot."

"Have you watched the video of the attack?"

Gillian stood. "I have."

She walked toward the basement door. I looked at Booster. He waved me down the hall. "Already seen it, and you're not going to learn shit from it."

When we got downstairs, Gillian replayed the incident on the computer. The various camera feeds flickered as they changed to earlier in the night. The parking lot cameras caught the arrival of the same white pickup. Again, the license plate was blacked out.

Three men in masks exited the truck. One guy grabbed a cinder block from the bed, spun around like he was in the Olympic hammer throw, and tossed it through the new glass window.

Gillian frustratingly motioned toward the monitor. "I should have put Plexiglas there. Something unbreakable." She shook her head.

"Why didn't you?"

"Because I never needed it before." She waved a hand around. "It's been fine up until now."

I pointed to one of the monitor feeds inside Sunshine Smiles. "Where was Rock?"

"In the bathroom."

As before, two of the guys used crowbars to clean the glass from the edges of the window.

There was a blur of motion on the tanning salon feeds as Rock entered the picture. He lifted the shotgun and fired twice. The men standing outside at the front of the store moved for cover. One of them wasn't fast enough. It appeared he'd been hit in the mid-section.

The guy who had thrown the brick removed a gun from his waistband. He fired three quick shots, and Rock went down.

Outside, the two masked men grabbed their fallen comrade and dragged him into the truck. The pickup sped away.

"That was a lot of gunfire for the cops not to show," I
said.

Gillian said, "Who's to call? The businesses around
here are closed."

"Someone from the mobile home park." I motioned
toward the back of the building.

"Maybe, but none have shown up so far."

"The gut shot is serious. They probably took him to an
emergency room. And if he's there, the cops will know."

Her face paled. "You think they still might show up
here?"

"I don't know. Maybe. But the guy was part of a
botched robbery. If he's alive and talking, he'll likely say
he was jumped. He'll create a story. I think you're fine."

She didn't appear convinced.

"What did you do about the blood on the front
sidewalk?"

"Booster got a bucket of water and washed it off."

I stared at the still video picture. "Whoever attacked
you is gonna come with bigger guns and more guys next
time."

Her brow furrowed. "Why do you think that?"

"At best, you put one of theirs in the hospital. At
worst, he's in the ground. They can't let that stand."

Gillian held her head in her hands. "Who is doing
this?"

"I don't know yet."

She looked up. "When will you?" It was a plaintive
whine.

"Hard to tell."

Gillian stood. "This is getting out of hand." She
headed toward the staircase, and I followed her.

Upstairs, all four of the Souls stood in the lobby.
Gillian approached Booster. "John thinks they'll make
another attempt."

The older biker eyed me. "Because of the guy Rock shot? Makes sense."

"When will this stop?" she asked.

"It won't," Booster said. "Until we know who's behind it." He considered me. "Isn't that right, Nancy Drew?"

The other bikers chuckled.

I faced Gillian. "Looks like you got things under control here. Call me in the morning."

"You're leaving?" she asked. "Don't we need a plan or something?"

I pushed open the back door and headed toward my truck. She followed closely. "Wait, John."

"Listen." I paused a moment to collect myself. I lowered my voice. "You might trust those guys in there, but I don't."

"Rock is my brother-in-law—"

"He's not anything to me."

I pulled open my truck door. She put her hand on my arm.

"Are you still working this?"

"If you're still paying double, I am."

She nodded.

"I'll check in tomorrow."

Gillian stepped back, and I pulled the door closed. She stayed in the parking lot until my truck crept back around the corner.

Chapter 11

Shortly before eight in the morning, I went back to Trevor Kobold's house on York Avenue.

After returning home from Gillian's building, I'd gotten a few hours of sleep. Then I took Corporal into the park for a quick game of ball. I would have liked a more leisurely morning, but I suspected drug suppliers weren't the type to rise early, and I wanted to catch them before they did.

In front of Trevor's home was the same Honda Passport as before, but now a newer Yukon Denali sat behind it.

I parked a couple of houses away. Before getting out, I tucked my gun into the back of my jeans.

As I walked up the sidewalk, the horde of gnomes watched me with static fascination. They seemed more disturbing at this hour as if they'd waited through the night for their first victim to arrive. The one waving at me was just asking for trouble.

I knocked on the door. A handful of seconds passed before I knocked again. When a decent amount of time went by, I pounded on the door. Finally, there were footsteps inside.

The same blond man from earlier answered. His hair was mussed, and his eyes were puffy. He held a yellow towel around his waist. "You again?" His voice was gravelly from the aftereffect of sleep.

"Is Trevor home?"

His face scrunched, and he clucked. "What time is it?"

"I'll wait here while you get him."

Before the guy could protest any further, another man entered the room. He wore only a pair of running shorts. He rested his hand on the other's shoulder. "Who's this?"

"The guy who was here yesterday."

"Trevor Kobold?" I asked.

"What about it?"

Kobold stood close to six feet tall. He had a slim build, shaggy hair, and no tattoos.

"I've got some questions for you."

"I look like Radio Shack? Get your answers elsewhere." He stepped back and said to the other man, "Close the door."

"Fine," I said through the narrowing gap. "The cops will be by to ask them."

That stopped the door just before it shut entirely. It slowly opened back up. Both Kobold and the other man remained in the entryway.

"Let's go back to bed," the first man whispered.

Kobold didn't listen to him. Instead, his face hardened. "Say that again." His tone sounded threatening, but it was hard to take him as a serious menace. Not only was he standing there almost naked, but a circus of gnomes guarded his house.

"If I leave here without answers, I'm gonna let the cops know about your operation. Then you'll deal with them."

Kobold glanced at his boyfriend, then returned his gaze to me. "What's your name again?"

"He said it yesterday," the boyfriend offered, "but I forgot."

I remained silent.

Kobold's lips pursed, and he exhaled forcefully through his nose. "What is it you want to know?"

"Remo Lightly."

He flicked his hand dismissively. "Ah, man, fuck that guy. He's back—What? A few weeks? —and someone shows up at my door. What's this about?"

"People getting hurt."

Kobold looked to his boyfriend again. "That doesn't sound like Remo." He eyed me. "You got the wrong guy."

"No, I don't."

"Then Remo is mixed up in it unwillingly."

"Which is why I need to ask you some questions."

"He gets what he gets." Kobold stepped back and grabbed the door. It started to shut.

"The cops," I said.

The door paused in its swing. Kobold stuck his head through the small opening. "Why me?"

"Because you're the guy with the answers." I looked over my shoulder. Across the street, a gray-haired man pretended to tend to some flowers. His attention was locked on us, though. "Maybe I can come inside? Looks like your neighbors are taking an interest in us."

Kobold craned his neck to check out his neighbor. "Goddamn, Herb." He stepped back and pushed open the door.

After I entered, I closed the door behind me.

The inside of the house was impeccable. It was in sharp contrast to the exterior of the home. Everything was in its place. The living room appeared freshly painted, and the furniture looked new. Framed artwork adorned the walls.

If the home's exterior looked nicer, would that call more attention to Trevor Kobold? Was he hoping to avoid the interest of law enforcement? Or the neighbors? Or drug dealers thinking he made too much money off them?

And if the guy wanted to avoid attention, what was up with all the gnomes lining his sidewalk?

Maybe Kobold simply rented the place, so he and his boyfriend only cared about the house's interior.

The boyfriend shifted his position, and his hand twisted the towel around his waist. He eyed me with disdain. "How long is this gonna take?"

"*Devin*," Kobold said.

The boyfriend's attention snapped to him. "*What?*"

"Put some clothes on."

"Why can't I be involved in this discussion?"

Kobold's shoulders slumped slightly. "Just do what I ask, will ya? And grab me a shirt while you're at it."

Devin rolled his eyes. "Whatever."

When the other man was out of the room, Kobold crossed his arms and frowned. "Thank you so much for the heartburn this morning. Like my life doesn't have enough drama in it."

"Sorry about that."

Kobold looked toward the ceiling. "So, Remo."

"How'd you know he was back in town?"

His gaze dropped to me.

"If you weren't supplying him anymore, how'd you even know he left?"

Kobold shrugged a single shoulder. "You know how it is. People talk. They've seen him around town." He scratched the underside of his jaw. "Why do you care so much about Remo?"

"I don't. He isn't my client."

This seemed to interest him. He shifted his stance and cocked his head slightly. "Are you a private eye or something? Like in the movies?"

"Investigator, and it's nothing like the movies."

"Except you're serious about the cops."

"As a heart attack."

Kobold inhaled deeply, held his breath for a moment, then let it free. He moved to the front window and looked out. I wondered if he was watching Herb tend to his flowers. "I treat my dealers fair, you know?" Kobold glanced back at me before continuing. "Not everybody can say that, but I can. I don't screw them over. I never short them, and I don't take more than what's fair. Understand?"

I nodded.

He faced me. "But in return, I expect loyalty. Not a lot. Not like a king, you understand. Just a little goddamned loyalty." He held his thumb and forefinger a millimeter apart. "Doesn't that seem fair?"

I nodded again. It seemed that's what he wanted to keep going. It was a low price to pay.

"I liked Remo. For real, no joke. Oh, I could give you some real Kumbaya shit about him being a good guy with a decent soul." Kobold motioned toward the back of the house. "That's Devin's realm. And Devin liked him, too. He'd tell you how he was born when Venus was in Pluto's orbit or some nonsense, but in my world, Remo was a good earner with lots of experience. I liked that. I also liked that he never complained. And he had a solid clientele. Doctors, lawyers, teachers, and such. Not high school or college kids. Fuck those teeny boppers. Remo's clients never complained about the product, they never stiffed him on a payment, and they never asked to spread their payments over time." Kobold pointed at me. "That's something a guy like me can appreciate."

"They were loyal."

He snapped his fingers. "That's right. Loyalty. That's all any of us wants, isn't it? Just a little loyalty." He held up his thumb and forefinger a millimeter apart again. "And why shouldn't those people be loyal to Remo? He'd been selling to them for years. Some of them since high school. Can you believe that? They basically grew up together. How cool is that?"

Kobold couldn't have been older than thirty.

I asked, "How long have you and Remo worked together?" The question sounded like something I would have asked a friend over dinner.

Kobold slowly smiled, then nodded. "I get why you're asking that. I'm so much younger than Remo, right? Me and Remo, we only go back a few years, but he worked with the guy I took over for. That's how legacy works. Legacy and loyalty. That's what business is built on."

"What happened to the other guy? The one you took over for."

"He had a—" Kobold's head bobbed from side-to-side while he thought. "Let's say he had an accident and leave it at that. Can we do that?"

"Sure." I wasn't investigating Kobold's rise to middle management.

"So Remo—" Kobold said.

It struck me as odd that he was willing to talk so freely when an uneasiness crept into my consciousness. Had Devin walked into the other room to get a gun? My right hand dropped toward my waist as Kobold continued speaking.

"We worked together well. At least, that's what I thought. No problems. Never an issue from him, and I never created one for him. Man, if we ever gave out an employee of the month, Remo would have gotten it so many times."

It's the same thing Remo had said. I glanced toward the hallway again.

Kobold tsked. "Then one day, he shows up, and bam! Just like that. Right out of the blue. He's done. Of course, I wanna know why. That's only natural. Don't you think?"

"Yeah, only natural."

My right hand was entirely behind my waist now and gripped the butt of my gun. If Devin popped out with guns blazing, he'd be the one surprised. I moved slightly to put Kobold between me and the hallway.

"Can you believe that Remo said he didn't want to sell anymore? After all those years? He gave some excuse that he'd pressed his luck for too long. Sounded like some bullshit that I should have called him on."

I asked, "Why didn't you?" just as Devin returned to the room. I saw the motion over Kobold's shoulder.

Instinctively, I stepped back to create extra distance, but there was no need. He didn't carry any weapons.

My hand released the gun and slipped from behind my back.

Devin appeared angry, though. He now wore a yellow tank top, black shorts, and flip-flops. He tossed a light blue t-shirt to Kobold as he passed by us. "Want coffee?"

"Yeah. Start a pot."

Devin threw a hand in the air. "What did you think I was gonna do?"

Kobold rolled his eyes. "He's going to be a bitch all day. Thanks for waking us at the crack of dawn." He unfurled the t-shirt and hollered into the other room. "Are you kidding me?"

"Just wear it!" Devin shouted back.

Kobold flapped the t-shirt twice before slipping it over its head. The logo on the front read *Bare Buns Fun Run*.

We stared at each other for a moment.

Kobold thumbed toward the kitchen. "It was his idea."

"Remo," I said, getting us back to the topic. "Why didn't you call him on his bullshit excuse?"

"I had this momentary thought that he was trying to get on the wagon and didn't want to be around the stuff. You know, that maybe he was afraid to tell me. That sort of thing has happened before. We're like any company. Everybody's got personnel issues. You gotta manage all sorts of crap you wouldn't believe. Baby-mama drama. Creditor issues. Blah blah blah. Anyway, people start thinking they should maybe stop smoking for one reason or the other, but they always come back. Usually, all I gotta do is bide my time."

"But it wasn't that."

"I also had this crazy thought—" He pointed at me. "—because this one happened, too. God's honest truth. I had this crazy thought that Remo found Jesus. I would never have expected that of him, but you know it could happen. I saw it all the time at my mother's church. Maybe Remo didn't want to risk his soul by selling the devil's weed anymore—that's what my mother calls it. Had that been the case with Remo, I would have respected it—I know how crazy the Lord's rules are because of my mother." He crossed himself and then kissed his fingers. Maybe he should teach Remo how to perform the sign of the cross.

"But you found out none of that was true," I said.

Kobold sucked in his cheeks as he eyed me.

"What did you do?"

"I followed him, like a jealous bitch. I'm not proud of it, but I wanted to know if he lied."

"You followed him? Not somebody else?"

His brow wrinkled. "Why? Me and Devin can't be private investigators?"

"What did you find?"

"We found the woman he dumped me for." Kobold shook his head. "That sounded catty, didn't it?" He looked into the other room. "Dev would have given me shit if he heard that. We found his new supplier."

"How'd you do that?"

"What do you mean how'd I do that?"

"Her operation isn't exactly out in the open."

Kobold walked over and dropped heavily into a leather chair. He playfully smacked both arms. "That's what this is about. Something's happened. You're working for her. Am I right?"

"How did you discover the operation?"

He waggled a finger. "You never said what your name was."

"John Cutler."

"John Cutler, the private investigator." Kobold crossed one leg over the other. His foot bounced with excitement. "We're at what they call an impasse, Cutler. Either you share with me, or you can take a hike. Now that I know who you're working for, you're not going to call the cops any more than I am."

I sat across from him in the other chair. "Someone attacked her operation."

Kobold interlaced his fingers and smiled. "That's great. Just great."

"Not really."

His grin widened. "And why's that?"

"Because the Wasted Souls are involved."

Kobold's smile faded. "The Souls? How'd they get involved?"

"She needed security, so she called them."

He unlaced his fingers and scooted toward the edge of his seat. "And now they see how this operation is running."

I nodded. "You see the problem."

"I'm starting to."

"How did you figure her operation out?"

Kobold waved a hand. "It wasn't that hard. I followed Remo. He'd enter the tanning salon and stay in there for twenty minutes. When he would leave, he'd never be any darker. Know what I'm saying?"

"Yeah."

"Then I watched him go back and do it all over again. Finally, I stopped watching him and started watching the building. Others came in regularly like Remo, but none of them ever got tanned. I watched the other businesses, too. You know what I noticed? They never got any traffic. None. No one ever came in to get anything printed or to get their nails done. It seemed to me that those businesses would have a hard time paying the rent that way."

He slid back into his chair and crossed his legs again.

"At first," Kobold continued, "I thought maybe the tanning salon was a distribution point. It was on Trent, easy to get to from anywhere, even some of those podunk towns in north Idaho, but I never saw anyone carry anything in. Like, no deliveries. Maybe I missed it. I wasn't there all the time, you know. Devin watched it some, but he said the same thing. Nobody ever delivered anything."

Kobold looked toward the kitchen. "How's that coffee coming?"

"You hear it gurgling?" Devin called back.

He eyed me. "Again, thank you for waking us up so early. He's gonna be like that all day."

"You were saying something about no one ever delivering to the building on Trent?"

Kobold leaned on the armrest. "Right. No deliveries. Devin went in once for a tan to check out the place. He said it looks like a legit business, but it doesn't operate that way. The girl at the counter said Dev couldn't get a tan that day because all the machines needed servicing. Can you believe that? *All* the machines? At *once*?" Kobold laughed to himself. "That's when we figured there must be a basement." He scooped his hand as if going under a table. "I wonder how many of those buildings around town have basements?"

"No idea," I said.

"After we figured there was a basement, everything else made sense. She was probably operating a grow down there. That's why guys like Remo showed up for a tan and left without getting any browner. It's a smart set-up. And I did the math. Figuring there's a full basement, she's growing anywhere from seventy-five to a hundred twenty plants. Can you believe that?"

I did my best to keep my expression flat.

"Nice poker face," Kobold said. "I'll give the lady credit. The tanning salon hides the power consumption while the other businesses mask the smell." His nose crinkled. "That rendering plant, too. Whew. Man, have you ever smelled that place?"

I shrugged.

He smacked the arms of the chair again. "I knew it. So sweet. The lady did all right."

"How'd you know the owner was a woman?"

"We looked her up."

I leaned forward. "You went to a lot of trouble."

"What can I say? We were interested."

Gillian's grow *was* discovered by a rival dealer, and she herself was found out. This was the leak, and it started with Remo. He might not have said anything, but how he ended the professional relationship with Trevor Kobold caused the man enough concern to follow him.

"What'd you do about it?" I asked.

"What *could* I do about it? It's not like I could run in there and steal the building. Maybe I was jealous, but I'm not that stupid."

Devin walked through the living room with a ceramic mug. "Coffee's done," he said icily. He continued back down the hallway.

"Bitch," Kobold muttered. His attention returned to me. "Who'd I tell? I wasn't about to tell my supplier."

"Why not?"

"Because they'd want me to get into some sort of pissing contest with her. Did business go down when Remo left? Of course, but that happens. Customers know dealers; they don't know me. When dealers go, sales dip. It dropped more than expected when Remo left, which pissed me off, but that's life. What wouldn't be good for business is starting a turf war that I could have avoided."

Kobold stood and stepped toward the kitchen. I stood to follow, but he stopped and faced me.

He said, "The Souls being involved is bad."

"I know."

"Bad for everyone."

"How so?"

"Here's what's gonna happen. They're gonna sniff the money she's making, and they're gonna want to take over. But you probably already expect that."

I said, "I have my concerns."

"Go with them. When that happens, we'll have a territory war. They'll wanna push out the little guys like me." He slapped his hands together. "I should have seen that happening."

"How could you have known the Souls would get involved?"

Kobold shrugged. "I couldn't. How did this lady even know how to contact them?"

"Her brother-in-law is one."

"Shit." He lowered his head. "Shit, shit, shit."

The leak, I thought. He discovered the grow, but he didn't tell his supplier. Yet, that didn't mean he didn't tell someone else.

"Who else knows?" I asked. "Besides you and Devin. It was too big of a discovery not to share. You couldn't keep that secret to yourself."

Kobold reached out and flicked the stitching on the back of the chair. "I might've told someone."

"Who?"

"A friend."

I waited.

Kobold looked up. "We're in the business. We play by rules, you know. Just like I was saying. Live and let live. He's got his piece, and I've got mine."

"What's this friend's name?"

He flared his arms. "I'll call him and ask if he told anyone. It's not like you're calling the cops."

"That's right. I'm not, but I'm gonna call someone else you fear a whole lot more."

"Who?"

"The Souls."

His eyes widened.

"They want to know who hit that grow, not once, but twice."

"It wasn't me."

"I'm going to say you've got a name that you're refusing to share."

Kobold held up his hands. "Hold on. The Souls are your client?"

I didn't answer.

"Jesus, man." He glanced around, then looked down the hallway toward where Devin had disappeared. "Why didn't you say so? We don't want any trouble. I thought you were working for her—what's her nuts? Not the fucking Souls." He rubbed his face. "If they want me out of business, I'm out. Like today. Tell them I won't make any trouble."

"They don't want you out of business. They just want the name."

Kobold nodded. "Yeah, yeah. Okay. The guy you want is named Karga. Yaban Karga."

"You told the Turk?"

"Why?" Kobold smiled. "You've heard of him?"

***

Standing next to my truck, I dug my keys out. My cell phone buzzed once—the signal I'd received a text message. I pulled the phone from my pocket.

NEED TO MEET U. ASAP. RIVERFRONT PARK. - G

I responded with a simple—K.

"I know what you're doing over there," a male voice said from behind me.

Herb tossed his little garden shovel into the dirt and stood with considerable effort.

"What's that?" I asked.

His silver hair was worn in a flat-top style favored by military men. His wire-rimmed glasses sat slightly cockeyed on his nose, and his jowly cheeks were flushed from either exertion or excitement. Herb wore a blue plaid shirt, brown shorts, and sandals over light brown socks. He angrily pointed a crooked finger toward Kobold's house. "I know what's going on over there. It's not right with the Lord."

He might have been talking about drugs or homosexuality, but I'm pretty sure it was the latter. I didn't care either way.

"Yeah, okay." I unlocked my trunk.

"Your soul is in jeopardy," Herb said.

I climbed into my truck and then faced him. "Hey, buddy."

He took a step forward and leaned in expectantly as if waiting for me to assail him with an insult or a slur. I wanted to tell him to shut up and to mind his own business. Maybe I'd even throw in an expletive or two. But what good was saying something like that going to do? He was already an angry bigot. I'd only be giving him another reason to hate. Kobold and his boyfriend hadn't done anything to me.

I lifted my chin in the direction of his garden. "Your flowers are beautiful."

That seemed to confuse him. "Huh?"

"Have a nice day." I closed my door. As I pulled away, I checked the rearview mirror. Herb stood in place and watched me leave the neighborhood.

Chapter 12

I was southbound on Division Street when my phone buzzed. It took a moment to dig it out from my pocket. Just as I flipped it open, the phone went silent. The screen showed the call was from Detective Gary Ackerman. I was about to dial him back when the phone buzzed again. I answered it. "Cutler."

"Sorry about that," Ackerman said. "I hung up just as you answered. I'm getting back about that thing you wanted."

I changed lanes to get around a slow-moving Chevy Astro. "The traffic stop." He must be at his desk and needed to talk in code.

"That's right. Took me a while to find it since I was basically looking for a needle in a haystack." He lowered his voice. "You're lucky I like you."

"I like you, too."

"Shut up."

I laughed.

"So, yeah, I think I found it. A red Mazda Miata was stopped back in July. That sound right?"

"Lines up with what I know."

"Okay, then I've got the incident number, and I'm looking at the call here. Uh…" He sounded distracted. I imagined him reading from a computer screen. "A county deputy initiated the stop. Looks like the driver was speeding. After they were stopped, the deputy ran the name. Driver came back with no warrants. A citation was issued for speeding. And then he cleared the call."

I looked over my shoulder and moved to the furthest left lane. The stoplight ahead switched to red, and I stopped. "That's it?"

"That's it. Just a routine traffic stop, as the newspapers like to say." His voice was almost a whisper. He was hard to hear, and I pressed the phone harder against my ear.

"Speak up," I said.

"What's this all about?" Ackerman asked.

"Was anything else mentioned in the report?"

"You're asking for too much." His voice was a whisper again. "You said all you wanted to know was the disposition of the call, and I told you more than I should have. What's going on?"

After talking with Trevor Kobold, I felt Yaban Karga was now a more viable lead than the deputy and driver involved in this traffic stop. That's how things are with an investigation. A path can be explored that quickly dead ends. Unfortunately, I asked for Ackerman's help which caused his ears to go up and his nose to go to the ground. He was interested now. I'd need to give him a story to satisfy his curiosity. It meant lying, which I didn't want to do. I liked the guy, but the last thing I needed was a cop—and a smart one at that—snooping around Gillian's business.

"Who was driving?" I asked.

"You're stepping over a line here. You know I can't tell you that." His voice changed as if he might be cupping a hand over the phone's receiver. "I stepped out on a limb by looking up the traffic stop."

"And I appreciate it, Gary. Was a man or a woman driving?" I felt bad for asking the question. Thi already told me a man was behind the wheel, but Ackerman's answer would set up my lie.

The detective waited a moment, then sighed. "A man, but I'm not telling you his name. No way."

"Anyone else in the car?"

"C'mon, really? What's up with the twenty questions?"

The light changed. As my truck rolled forward, I let the lie spill out. "A client hired me to follow her husband. It's been slow going on my end, but she thought she saw him in a red car with a woman. The woman was driving. I told her I would check it out."

Ackerman scoffed. "That's what this is about. Some skirt chaser?" His voice returned to normal. "Why didn't you say so from the beginning?"

I muttered the first thing that came to me. "Because you wouldn't have helped."

"You're damn right."

A thought came to me then. If the Yaban Karga lead didn't work out, I might have to circle back to this traffic stop. Perhaps the driver or the deputy were the ones really involved. But if the time came for that, I had a couple more pieces of information. It was a county deputy and a red Mazda Miata. I didn't want to ruin my relationship with Gary Ackerman over this. He already pointed out that we weren't the type of friends who spent holidays together, but we were the professional type. I needed to treat him as such.

"I'm sorry," I said.

"Yeah. Me, too. And who knows? If you were upfront about it initially and asked nice, maybe I would have looked it up and told you there was only a guy in the car. Saved us both some heartburn."

"I owe you one."

"And I'm going to collect."

"Coffee or beers?"

"Neither," he said. "You're coming over to dinner."

I almost rear-ended a Lexus and slammed my breaks. A car behind me honked.

"Are you serious?" I asked.

"Of course." Ackerman laughed lightly. "But not tonight. Look, I'll talk with my wife, and we'll get something set up. You want to be friends? This is what friends do. Talk with you later. I gotta go."

He hung up.

***

It took some time to find her. Riverfront Park covers a large area. We traded a couple of text messages until she led me to the right spot. I found her near the ticket booth for the gondolas. She was bent over with her face in her hands. When I sat on the bench next to her, Gillian straightened. Her eyes were red as if she'd been crying, but there was no wetness on her cheeks.

"Why are we meeting here?" I asked.

"It's close to where we first met." Gillian lazily motioned toward O'Doherty's.

"But why aren't we meeting in your shop?"

"We can't."

"Why?"

She swallowed with some difficulty as if holding back another flood of tears. "Booster is there with a couple of the club's girls. You should see them." Her face soured. "Raunchy. Tattoos up and down their arms. They look like they should be in prison, not a salon."

"What are they doing?"

"Booster's guarding the shop, but he's got those girls learning the business from Dawn."

I cocked my head.

She nodded. "He wants to take over the whole operation." She tapped her chest. "*My* businesses. Can you believe it? I called them for help, and this is how they repay me. He says the Souls will step in. Says it's in my best interest." She shook her head in amazement. "My best interest."

I suspected that something like this would happen. Now, the events were playing out as I discussed with Trevor Kobold.

"Are you going to let him take it?" I asked.

She angrily wiped at her eyes. "I don't want to, but what can I do to stop it? I'm me. Alone. Who's going to help me? You and what army?"

I stared at her.

"I didn't think so. That's my dilemma. So, Dawn's there now by herself."

"What's there to teach?"

Gillian threw her arms up in frustration. "Does it even matter? They'll take it over. It's mine. I built it. They can't come in and take it." She loudly clapped her hands together. "It's not fucking right!"

A young couple pushing two baby strollers looked in our direction. I waved at them. The husband nodded politely.

"You own the building," I said softly. "You also own the business. Legally, I would imagine."

"I do." She stood now and began pacing. "With LLCs and proper operating agreements and all sorts of other legal filings."

"Did you remind him of that?"

She spun and faced me. "Of course I did. Do you think I'm stupid?"

"No."

"I told him I have a mortgage, that I have expenses to run the building—" She ticked those items off on her fingers. "You know what he said? He said they'd pay me rent. *Rent!*"

"Maybe that wouldn't be so bad."

Her face contorted with rage. "Not you, too!"

"All I'm saying is that they would assume all the risk and—"

"No!" Her arms flailed about. "It's *my* business." She started walking away but stopped and returned. "You know, nobody helped me build it. Not my husband. Not Rock. *Me*." She banged on her sternum. "I'm not going to let anyone muscle me out."

Gillian turned and walked away. I thought she might stop and come back. When she didn't, I jumped from the bench and followed her.

"Hold on," I said. "Relax."

She slowed.

"Have you talked with Rock?"

Her face softened. "He's stuck. He's pissed that Booster is making this move, but what can he do? He can't go against the club's sergeant-at-arms."

"Is this a club decision?"

She shrugged. "Rock doesn't know. He's checking into it."

"Okay," I said. "Let's slow down here. You haven't agreed to this takeover, have you?"

"Are you crazy?"

"So, Booster has only proposed it."

"He's done more than that. He's trying to bulldoze me." She shook her head. "But he's got another thing coming if he thinks I'm going to roll over."

"We need to relax and think this through."

Gillian eyed me. "You need to stop telling me to relax."

"Let me talk with Booster."

"What do you think that'll do?"

"I don't know, but you want to keep your operation, don't you?"

She nodded.

I turned and headed southbound.

"Where are you going?" she hollered.

"To get a tan," I called over my shoulder.

***

It was strange to see the plywood back up on the window of Sunshine Smiles. I'd only seen what it normally looked like for a single day. I reached into the glove box and pulled out my gun. I slipped it into the back of my pants and hoped no one was watching the video camera in the basement.

When I entered the business, the electronic bell rang.

Dawn stood behind the counter. Her tanned skin and bleached hair were in stark contrast to the two women flanking her.

They both had black hair and pale skin. Each wore black t-shirts, and colorful tattoos ran down their arms. The women were moderately attractive in the way *Easy Rider* cover models were. Danger lurked within them, as did a healthy lack of self-respect. It was something I would have found highly alluring a few years ago.

All three women watched me when I entered.

Booster reclined in one of the nearby chairs. He thumbed through a *People* magazine.

The radio station no longer played top 40 pop music. It pumped out some annoyingly loud heavy metal song. I couldn't understand a single lyric over the grinding guitars and thumping drums.

"Look who it is," Booster said. He tossed the magazine to the floor and stood. He wore the leather vest bikers call a cut, a white t-shirt, and faded blue jeans. He pulled down on the vest to straighten it. "Find who's responsible yet?"

"Can we talk?" I motioned toward the front door.

His eyes narrowed. "Out back. You first."

We stepped into the rear gravel lot. Across the way, I could see the Park Estates Mobile Home Park. Xavia was out walking her cat. She noticed us and waved.

"Friend of yours?" Booster asked.

"I get around."

Booster moved and put himself between me and the park. I noticed the small patch above his left breast read *Sergeant-at-Arms*. "What are we doing out here, Cutler?"

"What's going on with the Souls and Gillian?"

"That's none of your concern."

"I've got a contract."

Booster's brow furrowed. "That's how it is, huh? You wanna make sure you get paid. You're just a sleazy salesman."

"I'm busting my hump while everyone else is sitting around."

He menacingly stepped forward. "Fuck you and your sitting around. One of my brothers got shot. What have you been doing?"

"Chasing leads."

"And where's that got you?"

"I'm seeing the plays being made."

Booster pursed his lips. "And what plays are those, tough guy?"

"Have you run this hostile takeover by the club?"

He cocked his head. "Best watch your tone."

"Why is someone with your stature in the club standing guard when a prospect would do?"

"Maybe we think this play is important."

I scoffed. "Sure."

"That tone, Cutler." Booster's face reddened. "It's starting to wear."

"How's Rock?"

"None of your concern."

"What's he think of you moving in on his sister-in-law's business? Can't be good for the brotherhood."

Booster punched me. I saw the wind-up and turned away. His blow glanced off my shoulder. I hopped back and lifted my hands in defense. I would have fought back in another situation, but not with the Souls. If you fight one man, you fight them all.

And there was no need to pull out my gun yet. It hadn't risen to that level of a problem.

Booster pointed. "Get out of here, narc."

"Listen."

He stepped forward again, and I moved back.

"Last warning."

"All right," I said.

I stepped toward the door.

"No." Booster snapped his fingers. "The long way around."

I moved toward the corner and stopped. He stood waiting at the back door.

"What?" he asked.

"What happens if the leadership doesn't want to take over the operation?"

"They will."

"Maybe they think it'll be too risky."

He flicked his hand in my direction. "I said fuck off."

"Got to be something to consider."

Booster stepped toward me. "You really want your head busted in, don't you?"

I lifted my hands in mock surrender. "Only a question." I backed around the corner. When he was no longer in sight, I headed toward my truck.

Chapter 13

The Turk wasn't at his apartment when I arrived, so I waited in my truck down the block. Maybe I should have asked for his phone number the first time I talked with him. Or perhaps I should have asked Trevor Kobold to give me the number.

Regardless, I knew who I needed to talk with now and where he lived. I could run around town asking folks if they saw him, or I could wait for Karga to return home.

I'd gotten good at waiting. Private investigation dealt a lot with that. Simply watching until someone did something. That thing might be sleeping with the wrong person, taking the wrong thing, or doing the wrong action.

One of the things that had helped me whittle away the time in the past was smoking. Now that I quit, I liked snacking—mostly salty stuff like sunflower seeds or pistachio nuts. But I didn't have any nuts right now. I would have been happy with something crappy like walnuts. I opened my notebook and made a list of nuts I would buy later and keep in the truck for impromptu moments like this.

Whenever someone appeared on the sidewalk, I lifted my head and felt my hopes rise. It had been almost an hour, and the Turk hadn't shown. Plenty of homeless folks walked by. Several prostitutes strolled past—not together but individually. Each of them took a particular interest in me. A man sitting alone in a vehicle sends a specific signal in this part of town.

Eventually, Yaban Karga showed up, or rather a blue Ford Explorer did. It pulled to the corner, and the Turk climbed out. After he cleared the vehicle, he closed the door and patted the vehicle's roof. The Ford accelerated away. Karga moved toward his building.

He wore another tracksuit—this one was red with white piping down the side. A black newsboy rode slightly cocked on his head.

I slipped from my truck, closed the door, and trotted across the street.

Karga unlocked the front door, pushed it open, and stepped into a small lobby. Before he could close the door, I was behind him, shoving him toward a set of stairs.

"What is this?" he said.

"We need to talk."

"No."

"Go upstairs," I said.

His face hardened, and he reached for his waist. It was a slow motion because he had to pull the tracksuit's jacket up. I punched him, and his hat slipped from his head.

Karga collapsed on the stairs, but he still managed to get the gun from his waistband. There wasn't anything for me to hide behind, so I reached for Karga's wrist and fell on the man in the process. He expelled a whoosh of air. "Oof!"

My hands wrapped around the gun. His free hand grabbed onto one of my arms.

I dropped an elbow into his face, and the grip around the gun loosened immediately. When I pulled it free, I pushed off him and stood.

Karga rubbed his cheek. "Why are you robbing me? What have I done to you?"

"I'm not robbing you."

"Yes, you are. Look." He pushed both of his hands toward me.

"Yaban, I came to talk."

He appeared confused. "But you hit me and took my gun."

"You pulled it on me."

"Because I didn't know what you wanted."

The gun was a hammerless .38 Smith & Wesson. I would have figured a guy like Karga to carry an automatic, but not everyone was comfortable around weapons. Perhaps this was an evil of his trade that he suffered.

Or maybe a heavier gun couldn't be easily hidden in the tracksuit, and he chose his weapon for fashion's sake.

I pressed the cylinder release and tilted the revolver. Five rounds fell into my open palm. When I jerked the gun, the cylinder snapped back into place with a satisfying click. I offered the revolver and rounds to Karga. "I apologize for the misunderstanding."

His brow furrowed in confusion. He hesitated for a moment, then stood to accept the items. He slipped the rounds into a pocket but clutched the .38 in his fist. "What do you want to talk about?"

"Trevor Kobold."

The Turk's brow wrinkled. "What do you want with him? We do not do business together."

"He told you about a grow operation."

His eyes flattened. "I know about many grows."

"The one on Trent."

Karga studied me now. "Let's go upstairs. Lock the door behind you."

I secured the door and followed him.

We didn't talk the entire two flights of stairs. Instead, we trudged up in the same rhythm. The stairwell was extremely wide, and the stairs were worn from a century of scuffing.

When we got to the third-floor landing, Karga slipped a key into a heavy-looking door. The lock opened with a quick twist of the wrist, and he pushed the door forward. From inside, a television played. It sounded like a game show.

Karga's shoulders slumped, and he grunted. He paused before stepping in. When he did, he shook his head and mumbled to himself in an unfamiliar language. He eyed me. "She is still here." He sounded defeated. "Why won't she leave?"

I followed him in and closed the door behind me.

His apartment was a wide-open space. The brick walls were exposed on each side. Wood beams crossed overhead. A toilet was in the opposite corner from where I entered, but no walls surrounded it. There didn't seem to be a kitchen.

Pizza boxes and bags from various fast-food restaurants were piled near the entry along with empty liquor bottles and beer cans.

The Turk moved deeper into the apartment. There was an unmade bed, a couch, and a TV. The game show host continued his obnoxious barking and insistence for the contestants to wager their earnings.

Even without air-conditioning, the space was comfortable. That was likely due to the brick walls and the only exposure from daylight being the north-facing windows.

Karga tossed the empty .38 onto the bed as he stalked toward the TV. His fingers slipped under the bottom edge of the television, and the screen went dark. Silence descended over the apartment.

The young blond woman I'd met on Sunday lay sleeping naked on the couch. Her face was buried in the crook of her arm. With the room suddenly quiet, I could hear her snoring. A needle, a cotton ball, and a bent spoon were on the floor.

The Turk stepped toward the couch and smacked the girl's butt. When she didn't move, his hand cracked her ass a second time. This one was harder.

"Liliya," he said sternly. "Wake up."

She stirred. "*What?*" She sounded like a surly teenager—probably because she still was.

"Go home."

"*Why?*" She hadn't opened her eyes yet and continued to speak into her arm.

"Because I said so."

Liliya didn't move.

Karga considered her for a moment. "I'm done with you."

She looked up now. "Nuh?"

"You no longer serve a purpose. Leave. Go."

Liliya bolted upright. "But I thought you liked me."

"I liked your friend better."

She stood now and pushed into Karga. Liliya didn't notice me or if she did, she didn't seem bothered by her nakedness. She touched the Turk's chest in a pleading manner. "C'mon, Yaban. Don't make me go. I like it here."

"You like my drugs."

Her hands caressed his arms now. "That's not true." She tossed her head from side to side like a child denying a parent's accusations. "I swear. I like it here with you. If you don't want me to use anymore, I won't. I promise. I'll be good." She dragged a finger over a breast. "Cross my heart."

Karga lifted an eyebrow. "Fine. Be of some use and get us some food."

Liliya noticed me for the first time. When she faced Karga again, she said, "Yeah. Okay. Sure." She unapologetically held out her hand. "Whatever you want."

He smirked but dug into his pocket, nonetheless. He pulled out a twenty and handed it to her. "The McDonald's. You know what I want."

She motioned toward me. "Am I getting him anything?"

"No," Karga said. "Now, go."

Liliya scooped up the same shorts and t-shirt I'd seen her wearing on Sunday. Had she been with Karga for three days?

She bent to look under the couch. "Where are my flip-flops?"

"Go!" Karga ordered.

Liliya straightened. "But I'll be in my bare feet."

"How is that my problem?" The Turk pointed toward the door. "Now!"

"Yaban," I said, but he held up a hand for me to stop talking. He watched Liliya as she padded toward the front of the apartment. At the last moment, she detoured toward the toilet.

"What are you doing?" he asked.

She sat and clutched her clothes to her chest. The money was clenched in her fist. "I gotta pee."

"No!" Karga said. He pointed several times toward the door. His face reddened. "Do that at the McDonald's."

"But I already started," she whined.

Karga's face reddened. "Liliya!"

"Yaban," I said again, but he pushed his palm in front of my face.

"Go now," the Turk said. "Before you never get another taste of—"

She stood. "All done." Liliya ran for the door. "I'll dress on the stairs. Have a good conversation."

"Flush the toilet!" Karga yelled, but the door closed behind her.

He turned to me with his lips pursed. "I apologize."

"Don't apologize to me. Apologize to her parents."

"For what?"

I pointed to the needle and the bent spoon.

"You want to judge, or do you want to talk? You can't do both." He took off the tracksuit jacket and tossed it onto the bed. He then plopped onto the couch and rested his arms along its back. There were no needle marks anywhere on them.

"You don't shoot up with her?"

Karga rolled his eyes. "I only sell the product. I would never put any of it in my body."

"But you let her—"

"Talk or judge," Karga repeated. His face hardened. "You can't do both."

I nodded. "I came to talk about Trevor Kobold."

"He is a good man. What do you want to know?"

"What did you do with the information he gave you?"

Karga's lip curled. "Why should I tell you anything? You come to where I live and judge me. You assault me."

"I already apologized for that."

"A misunderstanding, you said, but that is still no reason to tell you anything."

"What if I go to the cops?"

Karga's head lulled from one side to the other. "You think I'm scared of the police? Tell them. What are they going to do? Liliya can do as she pleases."

"I'm talking about the grow."

He chuckled. "You will tell the police about the grow? So be it. How does that hurt me? I know nothing."

"But that's not true."

"How can you prove it? How can they?"

"What about the Wasted Souls?"

Karga blinked several times before he pulled his arms off the back of the couch and tucked them into his sides. "What about them?"

"They are interested in that grow."

"Interested how?" A flash of concern passed over his face. "What does that mean?"

"They are out there now. I've talked with them."

He shrugged. "How does this bother me?"

"Someone attempted to hit it. Not once but twice."

Karga's eyes widened briefly. "That someone was not me. I had nothing to do with any robberies. Do not put that on me."

"How would I know you weren't involved? How would the Souls know?"

"Why do the bikers even care?"

"Because they are protecting the grow."

He leaned forward. "Like guards?"

I shook my head. "They were hired, but now they want to take over the operation."

Karga's eyes narrowed as if he were lost in thought.

"Someone with intentions to hijack that operation is a threat. You see what I'm saying, Yaban? I'm pretty sure you know how the Souls handle threats."

He jumped to his feet. "It wasn't me!" He waved his hands in front of my face. "Tell them! It wasn't me!"

"I need to give them a name. Yours is the only one I've got."

"That's not true. Who gave you my name?" His face pinched. "Trevor! That bastard. He told you about me? He is not so good as he seems. Give them his name."

"I already knew about you, Yaban. Besides, I like Trevor."

He continued to wave his arms as if he were warding off evil spirits. "But how could I do such a thing? I do not have any men. I work alone."

"You could hire some men."

"Bah!"

"A name, Yaban. Who did you tell?"

The Turk stopped waving.

"Either you tell me," I said, "or you tell the Souls, but you're going to tell someone. Believe me."

Karga's shoulders slumped. "But he will know."

"Who?"

He flopped back into the couch. "Surely, he will know if I tell."

"*Who?*"

Karga stared at his hands. "I lose no matter what I do."

"What's going on, Yaban?"

He rested his head on the back of the couch. "How could I know it would come to this? I couldn't. There was no way to know. Trevor, he must have known. The bastard. That's why he told me."

"He didn't know about the Souls. He's as afraid of them as you are."

Karga studied me. "He did not know?"

"If it makes you feel better, I threatened him the same way I'm threatening you."

He shook his head. "Why do you do this?"

"I need the truth, Yaban. As soon as I get it, I'll leave."

"And go to the Souls?"

"Unless you give me another name. Otherwise, I'll go to them."

Karga stared at his hands. It seemed as if he were trying to come to a decision. "We are competitors, you understand—Trevor and me. But we are friends because we do not steal the other's business."

"You're ethical drug dealers."

He frowned. "We only meet occasionally to share our woes. Do you understand? We never discuss our business. That is very important."

"I understand," I said.

"When he told me about the grow, I thought it was quite ingenious. The woman who put it together was very clever. Trevor didn't want to tell his bosses for fear they would want him to do something about it. He prefers others to do his violence."

"So, that's why he told you?"

Karga shrugged a single shoulder. "He thought maybe I could do something with it and that I would reward him for it." He rubbed his fingers together.

"Because you wanted to diversify into selling weed?" I again motioned toward the needle.

His smile was without humor. "I already sell that. No. I want to diversify into selling things other than drugs."

"Information?"

He nodded.

I thought of Deacon. I'm not sure what kind of living he'd carved out being a conduit to the whisper stream, but he seemed to be doing all right. Since I'd met him, he hadn't worked a job. I wondered if that's the type of thing the Turk wanted to do. Deacon had said that the Turk aspired to bigger things. Was this what he meant?

"You traded the information then."

He turned his palms upward. "Why risk freedom when you can get others to risk theirs for you?"

"How did it go down?"

"I traded the information in exchange for a finder's fee."

"That you'll split with Trevor?"

"Of course." A look of piousness crossed Karga's face. "I'm nothing if not fair."

"Who did you sell it to?"

"I should not tell you."

I leaned forward. "Tell me or tell the Souls. At this point, it no longer matters."

The Turk inhaled deeply. "You are not a nice man."

"That's been established."

His lips bunched together before he said, "There is a man in the city who does certain jobs like this—heists, they are called."

It was then I realized I'd been lied to yesterday morning. It felt as if the blood drained from my face.

"By the look on your face, it seems you already know this man."

"Say his name."

Karga stood. "Why should I do such a thing? It is clear you already know him. For me to say it now, there is no profit—only pain."

I punched the Turk, and he collapsed onto the couch. "The name!"

He clutched his chest.

I hoped Karga would continue to remain silent—to try and hold on to some sort of criminal code of honor. That way, I could hit him again. The image of the teenager using drugs bothered me.

But Karga robbed me of that satisfaction. "Double G," he croaked. "No need to hit me again. Double G is the one."

I pointed at the needle on the floor. "When that girl comes back, send her home."

Karga waved a hand. "Whatever you say."

I stepped back.

"But it won't do any good."

"Just do it," I said. "Make sure she goes home."

I headed toward the door.

"Why do you think she's here?" Karga called after me. "Liliya likes it too much."

Chapter 14

Tremaine Brown sat on a bench in A.M. Cannon Park, although his butt was on its back and his feet were on the seat. He watched as I approached across the large swath of grass. Corporal was by my side. When we neared him, I stopped and threw the tennis ball. The dog sprinted away.

"He'll bring it back?" Tremaine asked.

"Every time."

"You train him to do that?"

I shook my head.

Tremaine hopped down from the bench. "So, it's in his nature to bring it back."

"I'm not sure about that."

Corporal dropped the ball at my feet. I picked it up and offered the ball to Tremaine. He shook his head, so I hurled the ball once more. The dog raced away. "Corporal had an owner before me," I said. "I don't know if he taught him to play. Maybe he did."

"Dog seems to like it."

I eyed the younger man. "I'm happy to keep talking about my dog."

"Nah. You said there was a business opportunity."

"What do you do for the gang?"

He rolled his eyes. "Man, I thought we went over this. I'm not quitting and—"

I held up a hand. "You took my question wrong. Are there designated roles like in a company? President. Treasurer. That sort of thing."

Tremaine pinched his nose. "Like do we wear name tags and call the meetings to order and shit like that? No. But we have roles, yeah."

"And what's yours?"

"Grunt. Foot soldier."

"Cannon fodder."

He cocked his head. "Done with the jokes?"

"You're new. You haven't made your bones yet."

"Listen to you, Mr. Streetwise." He snorted. "I might be new, but I've done all right." It was said with the confidence of the young and inexperienced.

Corporal returned and dropped the ball. I tried to ruffle his fur, but he excitedly stepped away from my hand. His attention was on the ball. I bent and picked it up. He backpedaled several steps in anticipation of a throw. I hucked the ball, and the dog ran away again.

"I assume the Dead Boys deal."

Tremaine studied me.

"I'm not setting you up." I pulled up my shirt.

He flicked his hand. "If I thought you were, I wouldn't be here."

"Then what's wrong?"

"I'm waiting for the punchline."

"I asked about growers."

He shook his head. "Not this bullshit again. A hundred plants, right?"

"That's right, and it's the real deal."

"I don't believe it."

I tapped my chest. "I've seen it."

"In the middle of the city?"

"The valley, but yeah. A mini forest of marijuana. Right under everybody's noses."

Tremaine shoved his hands in his pockets. "What of it?"

"Would you buy from this supplier?"

He stiffened his arms, which pushed his pants down slightly. "Hell, if I know. Maybe. I don't make those decisions."

"Who does?"

He grew more suspicious. "Why are you asking?"

"The grow is a nice operation, but it's gotten noticed by the wrong people."

"The cops?"

I shook my head. "As far as I can tell, they're in the dark."

"Where they should be." That made him smile. "Who's keeping tabs on it?"

"The Wasted Souls."

"Those pale bastards," he muttered.

"And they're applying pressure to take it over."

"What's that got to do with us?"

"The Souls don't understand the parable of the golden goose."

"What'd you expect?" Tremaine's gaze drifted toward the community pool. A moment later, his attention returned to me. "What do you think? That those bastards are gonna take over the grow and run it into the ground? That the goose will stop laying its golden eggs?"

"I knew you were smart."

"Don't stroke my ego, Cutler. You want the Boys to get involved for some reason. Dispense with the bullshit and play your cards."

***

Stacy Mathers looked up from her computer when I entered her office. She was the bookkeeper for Up in the Air Roofing Company. Their office was in the industrial park just off Sullivan Road. She removed her reading glasses and stood.

"What are you doing here?" she asked. Her face registered concern as she looked toward the lobby.

I closed her office door. "I told the receptionist I was a high school friend and wanted to surprise you."

"She's not supposed to let anyone back."

"I tried to be charming."

Stacy smirked. "I'm sure."

"I need you to do something for me."

"If this is about last night—"

"It's not."

She glanced over my shoulder to her office window. "We can't do this here. This is my job."

I pulled an envelope from my back pocket. "I need you to hold this."

Stacy stepped around her desk. "What is it?"

"There's a letter in it."

She reluctantly reached for it, and tears welled in her eyes. "Are you breaking up with me?"

"If something happens to me—"

Now, her eyes widened. "What's going to happen to you?"

"Nothing. Everything is okay."

"But why are you giving this to me?"

"Just because. Now, listen."

She held the envelope like it was filled with plutonium.

"I'm going to meet with a man right now."

"What man?"

"A scary one."

"Who?" Her voice cracked with fear.

"This is my job. If something happens—"

"You just said nothing was going to happen."

I touched her arm. "Nothing is going to happen, but if it does—"

Stacy jerked her head. "What?"

"Take it easy. If I'm not back in two hours, I want you to open that letter and do what it says to do."

She stared at the envelope.

"Got it?"

Stacy nodded.

"I'm sorry, but you're the only one I could trust."

When I walked out to my truck, I stopped at the door. That wasn't true, I thought. She wasn't the only one I could trust. I could have given it to Sergeant Ackerman, but that would have meant going into deeper explanations. Maybe I could have given the envelope to Bosco, the owner of Club Royale. There were even others I could have gone to and asked them to hold a letter for a couple of hours.

I wouldn't have even needed the letter if Deacon wasn't sick. Just his name alone had bought me safety at the beginning of the summer, but I couldn't count on that now.

So why did I hastily scrawl that letter and deliver it to Stacy?

I knew the reason why.

And it wasn't one of trust.

***

Gary Gaspar leaned against the door jamb while his musclebound security man frisked me.

"This isn't necessary," I said, but I knew it was.

Double G hadn't gotten to where he was by being foolish or trusting. When I helped Remo solve his problem after their heist, I'd learned all I needed to know about Gary Gaspar.

We were at Gaspar's office, a warehouse just off Freya and Riverside. There was a small lobby and two offices. The rest of the warehouse was wide open and filled with cars, furniture, and pieces of construction equipment. There was even a pinball machine.

Trace roughly ran his hands up and down my legs. He carefully checked around my ankles. His hand cupped my testicles, then ran backward—it wasn't sexual. It was all business.

"Clean." Trace righted himself and shoved me away.

Gaspar pushed off the door jamb and slid his hands into his pockets. He wore a light-blue collared shirt, black slacks, and laced shoes. He looked like he could just as quickly step into a board meeting as run a criminal empire. Maybe that was the point. "What's this about, Cutler?"

"Can we talk in private?"

"Just because you're unarmed doesn't mean I trust you. Trace stays." He motioned toward his office. "But if you'd like to sit, then do so. We're civilized men, after all."

The latter wasn't true. There were enough stories out there about the violence that Gaspar had perpetrated.

I entered the office and sat in front of his large, dark-wood desk. Nothing was on it but a notepad, a pen, and a cell phone. On the walls were several framed pieces of abstract art.

Double G moved behind the desk and sat. Trace stood just in the periphery of my left eye.

"Lay it out, Cutler, but be quick about it."

"You know about Gillian Brewer's grow."

Gaspar grabbed the pad of paper and pulled it to him. He picked up the pen and clicked its nib into place. "Start again. Who are we talking about?"

For a second, I worried that maybe he didn't know, but that was just Gaspar screwing with me. He was simply continuing his charade. "You know her name, G. You know where she grows, and I know that you know."

Several seconds passed before Gaspar said, "You don't know shit about what I know, Cutler."

"Your guys hit it a few nights ago, and then they hit it again."

Double G didn't move, but Trace shifted his stance. I caught the motion in the corner of my eye. That didn't make the boss happy. I'm sure they would discuss it after I was gone.

Gaspar clicked his pen a couple of times. "I don't know what you're talking about."

"The three men doing the job didn't know there was a security door on the first attempt, so they came back prepared for the second. They were armed that time, so maybe they knew about the man waiting inside. However it went down, one of yours got shot in the gut. Their man took a round in the shoulder."

Double G tapped his pen against his notepad. His gaze fell to the desk. He seemed lost in thought.

I continued. "All that says to me is poor preparation. At first, I thought that was unlikely for a guy like you until I remembered you hired Remo."

Gaspar looked up. "Tread lightly, Cutler. You know about the situation because Remo asked for your help. It was an ill-advised move for many reasons, and you got lucky you found a resolution. If you're going to spout off about it, we might have to do something."

"I'm not spouting off," I said. "I'm asking what's changed out there."

He tossed his pen onto the notepad. "I'm going to say it again—I don't know what you're talking about."

"C'mon, Double G. What's going on out there that would lead a man like you to hire the Remos of the world?"

Trace shifted again. This time Gaspar didn't notice or, at least, he didn't care. He scratched below his right ear and studied me. "The Remos of the world. That's a good way of putting it."

"We can call them unprofessional if that's better."

Gaspar shook his head. "Your point was made." He leaned forward and rested his arms on the desk. "You really wanna know what's changed? It's the landscape—right beneath our feet, and we didn't even notice it happening. What do you think of that?" He glanced toward his security man, and they shared a knowing look. "And it's not because the Russians or the Asians are moving in. As far as I'm concerned, there's plenty of pie for everybody. If we stay out of each other's way, we can all make a living—and a decent one at that."

"Then what's the problem?" I asked. "I'm not seeing it."

Gaspar fell backward into his chair. He inhaled deeply. "The problem, if it can really be called such a thing, is that things have been too good for too long. Prosperity is making us weak."

Trace nodded. He appeared to have heard this argument before and was in complete agreement with it.

"How is prosperity a problem?"

Gaspar pointed outside. "The world is getting fat, dumb, and lazy. It started with that goddamn internet—the revolution that got everybody up in arms. Now, everybody's got access to more information than they know what to do with."

Before I could ask why that was a bad thing, Gaspar answered my unspoken question.

"All that information does is clog people's brains and stops them from thinking. They start looking around and wondering how come their life isn't as good as the next guy's. No one can be satisfied with what they got anymore. You heard about this thing called—" Gaspar eyed Trace. "What's it called?"

"MySpace," the big man said.

"So stupid. People are on it, sharing pictures of themselves, doing all sorts of stupid shit."

Trace shifted his stance. "They call it social media."

"Social, my ass." Gaspar waved his hand in the air. "They're on a computer making love to themselves. It's digital masturbation, the freaks."

"What's that got to do with your guys?"

Double G thunked the desk with his finger. "Not just my guys. The whole damn world, Cutler." He picked up his cell phone and slammed it down. "Everybody wants to be connected. Everyone wants the quick buck."

I thought that was a funny sentiment from a career criminal like Gaspar.

Trace clarified Double G's statement. "Some of our guys are staying home to day trade."

Gaspar pointed at his security man. "Know what that is, Cutler? Grown ass men, playing on their Nintendos, selling pieces of a company they don't give two shits about." He slapped his desk. "If I could smack a bat across the kneecap of the guy who came up with that idea." His chair slammed forward. "And don't get me started on those little pricks who think they can be real estate agents. They all want to be goddamned flippers now. You know why?"

I shook my head.

"The TV. There's a whole network of shows for nothing but fixing up a home and selling it. I don't even know what it's called, but they should call it like it is and name it the Fag Decorating Network."

Trace chuckled and muttered the network name.

"That's pretty good, right?" Gaspar eyed me. "You're not laughing."

Correcting a man like Double G of his homophobia wasn't done. In this moment, not only did he have the power, but he had the information I wanted. He needed to rant himself out of steam before I could get back to my questions.

He smirked. "Whatever. The problem, Cutler, is that no one wants to get their hands dirty anymore. Even my sister's husband thinks he's some flipping wunderkind now. Buy and sell, buy and sell. That son of a bitch is going to get his ass burnt, but what do I know? I'm just the asshole who runs a used furniture warehouse." He looked toward Trace and shrugged.

"I hear you," the big guy said.

Gaspar jammed his finger onto the desk again. "But when, not if, *when* the market turns, who do you think that idiot brother-in-law is going to turn to for money? That's right. Me. The guy who has continually kept his hands dirty." Gaspar paused and stared up at the ceiling. "So, that's the problem, and you won't hear that honest answer from those talking heads on the news. Too much prosperity. Too many good times. When anybody can make money quickly, nobody will work hard for it. What we need is a good old fashion recession. You know, something to remind people of what it's like to work."

"There are still a few people who are willing to get their hands dirty," I said.

Gaspar smirked. "The few who will are already in positions where they can't be risked." He motioned to the big guy. "Like Trace over there. I wouldn't risk him on any job. He's too damn valuable."

Trace's face remained impassive.

"So I'm left building patchwork crews. Bring a guy in from there. Grab another guy from over there. I don't like it. But I do the best I can and build it the best way to cover my ass. Sometimes that means extra layers of separation from the job. You know, so I can't get any blowback. Sometimes, yeah, sometimes we end up with a Remo in the ointment."

"Things worked out fine with Remo."

Gaspar nodded. "In the end, yeah, they did, but because of you."

"Back to this grow," I said. "You're the one who hit it."

"Did I say that? I never said that." He glanced at Trace, then back to me. "You said that."

Frustration tickled my chest. "If you want to pretend you don't know, run with it. But why didn't your crew know about the man inside?"

He stared at me.

I thought back to what he said—extra layers of separation. "You weren't involved in the planning. You found out about the job. You put together some guys and sent them after the grow. Were they experienced hitters?"

Gaspar's tongue worked something out of his teeth.

"Is the guy who got shot alive?"

Now, Double G turned his right hand over to inspect his fingernails. He wasn't going to admit to anything.

I glanced at Trace. The big man shrugged. My attention returned to Gaspar, who patiently waited for me to continue. I'm not sure what I expected from him. He was a professional crook. I wasn't going to waltz in here and get him to blather on about a secret space laser as if he was some James Bond villain. I needed a different approach.

"You don't have to tell me anything," I said, "but I'd recommend you call off your guys and walk away from this job."

He raised an eyebrow.

"Otherwise, it's going to get very bloody for you."

"You're threatening me?" Gaspar's face hardened.

Trace stepped toward me. I held up a hand for him to stop. "It's not a threat, G. It's some free advice."

"I never trust anything that's free. Not free food, free pussy, and definitely not free advice."

"You can trust this. The Wasted Souls are now involved with the grow."

Gaspar slowly leaned back in his chair, and his face tightened.

"They're providing security," I said.

"How did that happen?"

"The woman who owns the grow is related to one of them."

There was a flicker of something in Gaspar's eyes—anger or disappointment. It was hard to tell because the flash was so quick. He reached out and put a hand on his desk.

"This development," I said, "is not good for whoever is pulling the heist."

Gaspar's face soured. "Obviously."

"It's also not good for the woman who owns the grow."

He nodded. "She invited the wolf into the hen house."

"Moves are being made to force the wolf back onto the street."

Gaspar cocked his head. "How can that happen? The wolf is already in."

It wasn't a done deal. I hadn't even convinced Gillian to listen to my pitch yet. But I needed to get Gaspar to back off before anything else could be done. So, I laid out my plan. "The Dead Boys will become her exclusive dealer. They'll buy everything she grows."

"At a discount, I'm sure." He smiled now. "And if the Souls screw with the grow, they mess with the Dead Boys."

"And the Dead Boys can't get too eager and take her out because they'll run into the Wasted Souls."

"They'll still provide security then?"

I nodded.

"Is this your doing?"

"I'm just a lowly private investigator."

His lips pursed. "Who's mixed up in this how?"

"I was hired to find out who attacked the grow."

Gaspar eyed Trace, and the big man pulled out his gun. I expected that to happen sooner or later. There were certain moments in this life when the chips must be pushed into the middle of the table. This was one of them.

Trace put his gun near the side of my head.

"And who have you told about what you discovered?" Double G asked.

I raised my hands. I was still seated. There was no way to overpower Trace without getting shot. Today, words were my weapon.

"Before Trace does something stupid," I said, "you should know there's a letter in a sealed envelope."

Gaspar lifted a hand toward Trace. "If you're gonna tell me it's with Deacon, don't bother. The man is sick. He's no longer a threat."

"It's with a woman."

His eyes narrowed. "The woman who owns the grow?"

"A different woman. My woman. She's holding it for one hour. If she doesn't hear from me, she's to deliver it to the Souls."

Gaspar's face flattened. "Not the cops?"

"If you hurt me, G, I want revenge, not justice."

He inhaled deeply, then waved Trace away. "The Souls and the Boys are a serious complication."

"If you know who is behind the break-ins—"

Gaspar covered his heart. "I honestly don't know of what you speak, Cutler. Please pass that along to the Souls if they should ever hear my name."

"I will."

"But—" Gaspar laid his hand on his desk and affected the best look of contrition he could muster. "I promise to look into the matter. If I find out who's behind the break-ins, I'll let them know they are stepping into now hallowed ground."

I stood. "That's all that can be asked." I moved toward the door.

"Cutler," Gaspar said.

"Yeah?"

"Thank you."

I nodded. "Sure."

"What do you think is fair?"

"For?" I asked.

"Your advice about the Souls." Gaspar appeared serious. "I do appreciate it. What do you want in return?"

"I don't want anything."

Gaspar looked at Trace, then faced me again. "Nothing?"

"You and me, Double G, we're square. I'm sure we'll cross paths again in the future."

"Undoubtedly, but I pay my debts."

"Then consider this something I did for a friend." I opened my hand and stepped forward.

Did I want Gary Gaspar as a friend? No. But it was a hell of a lot better than having him as an enemy. I'd now run across him twice in less than a year. Maybe I would never see him again, but I figured being nice wouldn't cost me much. Besides, I wanted him to remember me as a guy not motivated by cash. Everyone around him probably asked for money in one way or another.

Double G stepped around his desk and shook my hand. "And you can discreetly let the grower know there won't be another attempt on her establishment." He pulled me close. "But keep my name out of your mouth. Understood?"

The menace in his voice was unmistakable.

Chapter 15

"I'm not doing that," Gillian said.

"You don't have to. It's your decision."

We were at the Denny's on Argonne Road, just off Interstate 90. I asked to speak to her away from the tanning salon, and that's the location we settled on. She started to sip her cup of coffee but put it down untouched.

It was late afternoon, and the restaurant was busy with the early-bird crowd. Most tables were filled with gray-haired couples. Metallic clanging and raised voices came from the kitchen. Servers bustled from table to table. The smell of cooked meat hung in the air.

Overhead, "Sunglasses at Night" played. I had no idea who sang it. Outside our window, northbound traffic lined up on Argonne Road. Southbound cars raced for the freeway.

"How could you do that without asking?" Gillian said. "What if I don't agree?"

I shrugged. "Then nothing. I didn't tell them who you were or where your grow was. I only told them you had a hundred plants and that the Souls were forcing themselves on you."

"But these guys are a gang, right? They'll figure out who I am."

"If you don't want to work with them, they're not going to make a stink about it, especially with Booster and his friends in the mix. They don't need to get into some pissing match that'll catch the eyes of the cops. From what I understand, this group is about doing things under the radar."

She sipped her coffee. "Under the radar. I like that."

"I figured you would."

Gillian set down the white mug. "Why are you doing this?"

"You hired me."

She waggled a finger. "I hired you to find out who hit my grow, which you haven't done, by the way."

I stared into my black coffee.

"Are you telling me you have?" Her voice was filled with disbelief. "When did you figure it out?" Gillian glanced around, then leaned in and whispered, "Who was it?"

"I can't say."

She fell back in her seat. Surprise crossed her face. "What the hell?"

I turned my coffee cup in circles. "Here's the thing."

"There's not a thing." Gillian's face reddened. "I'm paying you. That means you work for me. You're supposed to tell me this kind of stuff."

I met her gaze. "The group behind the attacks didn't understand the rules."

"There aren't any rules to what I'm doing."

"Sure, there are. There are rules to everything."

Gillian raised an eyebrow. "Enlighten me."

"You're an independent, and that means you're fair game. Then you became off-limits."

"I'm still independent. Nobody owns me."

I shook my head. "You stopped being independent when you called the Souls."

"I called Rock, not his club."

"He's a member of that family. Those are the rules."

She lifted a hand in frustration. "How was I to know?"

"Ignorance of the law is not a defense." That was a line I'd thrown out many times while in uniform. "Once you brought the Souls in, you became affiliated. That changed the game. Understand?"

"But I don't want to be affiliated."

"Tough shit. You are now."

Gillian frowned as she ran her finger around the lip of her mug. "I thought all the guys would be like Rock."

"Most are probably more like Booster than your brother-in-law."

She pushed the cup away. "It seems all the men in my life are trying to control me."

"I'm not trying to control you, Gillian. I'm trying to protect you. Do with it what you will."

"But you're saying if I don't want to lose everything, then I have to do what you're proposing."

I rested my arms on the table. "You can do something else. I don't know what that looks like, but you can't go to the cops." A thought occurred to me. "That's not true, you most definitely can go to the cops, but you jam yourself up in the process."

"Cut off my nose, so to speak."

"Maybe that's what you want."

"No, thank you. I like my nose."

"I'll be honest," I said. "I haven't given this a lot of thought. Maybe there's another course of action out there that I can't see. This opportunity presented itself, and I took a shot."

"With the Dead Boys." Gillian scrunched her nose. "What a name."

A server approached with a carafe of coffee. "Refill?"

Both Gillian and I pushed our cups toward her. While she poured, the woman asked, "Ready to order?"

"We're just having the coffee," I said.

Gillian nodded in agreement.

"All right," the server said, "but I'll be back to check on you in a few. Just in case you change your mind."

We pulled our cups back.

"So, these Dead Boys," Gillian said. "What do you know about them?"

"Not much. I know one of their soldiers is all. Seems like a decent kid."

"Who's in a gang?"

I shrugged. "Nobody's perfect."

"How did you meet him?"

"He's a friend of a friend."

Gillian studied her cup of coffee. "Can you trust this kid, this soldier?"

"I trust my friend, and he trusts the kid. That's good enough for me."

She stuck her tongue under her lip. "How do we go about setting up a meeting?"

"It's already done."

I motioned toward the other corner of the restaurant. Gillian followed my gaze.

Sitting in the far booth were Tremaine and another black man who seemed to be in his late twenties. Tremaine lifted his chin in acknowledgment. I returned the gesture.

"That was fast," she said.

"They're waiting for you. The younger guy is Tremaine. He'll introduce you."

"You're not coming?"

"This is your deal. I'm not invited."

She considered my words then eyed Tremaine and his associate once more. Gillian sipped her coffee a final time and then slid out of the booth. "All right," she said. "Let's see what these guys are willing to offer."

Gillian confidently walked over to the table and introduced herself. Overhead the Bangles sang about walking like an Egyptian. Someone dropped a plate in the kitchen, which produced an awful racket. Several customers turned toward the sharp noise, but I kept my eyes on Gillian and the Dead Boys. Once the introductions were over, Tremaine slid out of the booth and joined me.

He lifted his eyebrows in silent acknowledgment.

"I thought you'd stay over there," I said. "Maybe be part of the negotiations."

"Soldiers don't negotiate."

"Who's that who came with you?"

Tremaine looked out the window. "Janarius."

"Looks like he's been in the game for a bit."

His gaze returned to me. "You're doing that thing you do."

"Which is what?"

"Acting like a cop."

It was my turn to stare out the window. I watched the nearby traffic light turn green. The waiting cars began to move.

Tremaine said, "Someday, I'm gonna run this crew."

I studied him.

"Believe it."

"I thought you were in the Dead Boys because of your brother."

He shrugged. "Doesn't mean I can't be good at something."

Janarius and Gillian seemed to be having a productive conversation in the far booth. There were frequent nods and an occasional half-smile.

The server returned with the carafe of coffee. She seemed confused by Tremaine's presence. Her gaze drifted to the other booth and back. Maybe she'd seen people trade tables like this before, or perhaps she'd figured out we were working a deal. Or perhaps she just didn't care. She lifted the pot and eyed me. "Refill?"

I pushed the cup toward her.

As she poured, she glanced at Tremaine, "What about you? You hadn't ordered at the other table."

"Nothing, thank you."

She smiled and nodded.

"Want something to eat?" I asked.

Tremaine shook his head.

I looked up at the server. "Thank you."

"I'll be back in a bit to check on your cup."

Tremaine and I both turned to look outside. It seemed safer than staring at each other.

"It's gonna be a rough life," I said.

He lightly scoffed. "You wanna save me, Cutler?" His attention followed a sizeable black pickup as it drove northbound. "Maybe give me some white savior speech." Now, his eyes flicked to me. "You know the kind of talk. All I gotta do is apply myself, and I could be anything I want."

I stopped pretending to care about the traffic. "You already know your path. I'm not talking you off it."

He leaned his head back against the booth. "Then what are you trying to say?"

"What do you know about the police?"

His lip curled. "They're dirty."

"Not all of them."

"Enough to matter."

I shrugged a single shoulder. "Nothing you can do about it."

"The hell do you mean by that?"

"You can't change the world, and you can't change the system."

"You're a ray of sunshine." He grabbed the salt and pepper shakers. He absently banged them together.

"That's you and them."

He looked up.

"The cops and you," I said and motioned toward the shakers.

Tremaine understood then. He slid the shakers back to where he'd gotten them.

"It's always going to be that way," I said. "Nothing is going to change the game."

"You're not telling me anything we don't already know."

"So be nice when you can."

He grimaced.

"Cops like nice."

Tremaine glanced toward the other customers before leaning in. His eyes burned with hatred. "You telling me to be a rat?"

"No. Never. What I'm saying is be nice."

He flicked his hand.

"Nice goes a long way."

"Fuck nice."

"If everybody on the street treats a cop like shit, who's he gonna remember?"

Tremaine glanced at Janarius. "That doesn't make sense."

"It's human nature. Take it or leave it. No skin off my nose."

His attention returned to me. He didn't say anything for several beats. Eventually, he asked, "Nice?"

"The next time a cop talks with you, and you know there will be a next time—"

"No shit." He frowned, and his eyes challenged me.

"Be cool."

"Be cool," Tremaine mocked. "Like you're James Brown or something."

"Like I said, take it or leave it. I don't care."

There was motion in the far booth. Both Gillian and Janarius slid out. When they stood, the two shook hands.

She turned and headed in my direction. Janarius walked out of the restaurant.

"Peace," Tremaine said. He slipped out and passed Gillian on the way toward the exit.

Gillian dropped into the seat across from me. She seemed oddly serene.

"Everything okay?" I asked.

She nodded. "I'll tell you about it in a minute. Right now, I'm starving." She waved at the server.

***

Gillian beat me to the parking lot of Rosie's Bar and Grill. The establishment sat east of Pines Road and Trent Avenue. We could have had this meeting in the tanning salon, but it was better to do it in public.

We arrived at nearly seven, so the after-work crowd had filled the bar. The patrons seemed to be primarily employees from the nearby industrial park and production facilities.

Neon signs scattered about the bar's walls gave the interior an oddly blue glow. We found an open table—a tall, round one with four chairs—and sat. All the other tables were filled.

Near the door stood a jukebox. Bob Seger's "Night Moves" played overhead.

The bartender—a small woman in a tight, red t-shirt and jean shorts—approached. "What can I get you?"

"Three beers," I said. "Our friend will be with us in a minute."

She nodded and headed off.

The front door opened and bathed the bar in sunlight. Booster stepped in and looked around. Gillian lifted a hand. He noticed her, took a step, then paused. His face hardened when he saw me. The door closed behind him and took the sunlight with it.

"What's he doing here?" Booster asked as he slipped onto a stool.

"He's here because I asked him."

Booster leaned in toward Gillian. He lowered his voice so the neighboring tables couldn't hear him. "I thought we were going to discuss how things are going to be."

"We are," she said.

Like an idiot, I nodded in agreement.

Booster started to say something, but the bartender returned with several pint glasses. She held them like a triangle. Booster pulled back and allowed the woman to slide the beers onto the table. He scowled while he waited.

"Hey," she said to Booster, sliding a glass in front of him. He didn't bother to smile or acknowledge her.

She announced a total, and I handed her a couple of bills. "Keep the change."

"I'll be back in a bit to check on you."

When she walked away, I slid my beer to the side. Booster and Gillian did the same.

"So," Booster said. He leaned in and once more lowered his voice. "It's agreed. The Souls will take over the operation, and you'll act as landlord. Easy peasy."

Gillian shook her head. "No."

His brow wrinkled, and he glanced around. When he looked at her again, he said, "The fuck do you mean no?"

"My mother taught me that no means no. What about yours?"

Booster's lip curled as he considered me. "You did this."

"You should hear her out," I said.

He slipped off the stool. "You just screwed up, lady."

"Hey, Booster," I said.

"What?"

"Look over there." I lifted my chin toward the corner of the bar.

His eyes tracked my gaze. Standing with his left arm in a sling was Rock. He raised his right hand in a tentative wave. I would have liked a more forceful announcement of his presence, but it would have to do.

Booster's head whipped back to us. "What's he doing here?"

"We invited him."

"He's not sitting at this table. I'm the sergeant-at-arms. Not him."

"That's right," I said. "He's just muscle, but he already knows the terms of this deal, and he thinks it's a good one."

Booster scowled. "What's he know? Nothing."

"She's about to make you an offer. If you don't know what it is, who's going to look more in control back at the clubhouse? You or Rock?"

His jaw flexed. "You're fucking with me."

"We're trying to put a deal together. And Rock is trying to make sure his sister-in-law stays protected like the club offered in the beginning."

Booster swallowed. His eyes darted left and right. It seemed as if he were looking for a way out of his predicament. Eventually, his face relaxed, and he turned on his stool.

"What's the offer?"

Gillian leaned in. "I now understand how lucky I got with my operation."

Booster chuckled. "You think?"

"I ran it with too much kumbaya," she said. "I thought the only force I had to worry about was the cops. I should have had security all along."

"Security?" Booster glanced about before leaning in once more. "That's all you want us for?"

"Why not?" I said. "That's what you agreed to do. Besides, isn't that what you guys provide for other operations? Or am I wrong?" I knew I wasn't. While on the Seattle Police Department, I remembered hearing that the Seattle chapter of the Wasted Souls provided security for guns, human trafficking, and drugs. If someone needed muscle, the Souls were there to provide it.

"That's not the point," Booster said.

"That *is* the point," I said. "The Souls are good at security. How much do you know about growing?"

He pursed his lips. "We'd learn."

Gillian took a deep breath as if to steel herself. "Not in my building and not with my plants."

"Lady," Booster said. He didn't bother to lower his voice. "We'll take what we want, when we want, how we want. You don't know who you're screwing with."

Several customers looked in our direction.

Gillian remained silent and simply stared at him.

Booster seemed content with his outburst. "And bringing along your brother-in-law—" he thumbed over his shoulder "—didn't do nothing but put his ass in hot water."

I lowered my voice. "Better think about the Dead Boys before you do something stupid."

Booster blinked. "What?"

Gillian said, "I've entered into an exclusive distribution agreement with them."

"What are you talking about?" Booster asked. His head swiveled as he looked between Gillian and me. "The hell is going on here?"

"The Dead Boys are now my exclusive dealers. What I grow, they sell."

Booster slapped the table. "Where's that leave us?" he hollered.

Everyone in the bar looked in our direction.

I picked up my beer. "Drink."

Gillian lifted her glass and sipped.

Booster was slow to realize how many folks were watching us. When he finally did, he picked up his glass. He motioned a toast, then gulped down half the beer. He wiped his mouth with the back of his hand.

We sat quietly and stared at each other as the jukebox belted out Tom Petty's "Refugee." I looked into the corner to see Rock intently watching us. He raised a shoulder in a questioning manner. I shrugged slightly and turned my attention back to Booster.

"What's it going to be?" I asked.

"You fucked us," he said.

Gillian set her beer to the side. "I'll give the Souls a permanent gig if you want it. It's a cut into my profit. Trust me, it's not something I want to do."

Booster stared into his half-empty glass. "Lay it out."

"Someone is always on-site. Maybe not at night because I think the attacks will stop." She looked at me, and I nodded. "So, just when the doors are open."

"Where do you want us?" Booster asked. "Inside the tanning salon is gonna look odd. More than a little suspicious."

"Not the salon."

Booster shook his head. "And no way my boys are sitting with that freak in a gas mask. Those chemicals are hazardous."

Gillian lifted a hand. "Here's what I'm proposing. We'll change the nail salon to a tattoo parlor."

"An ink joint?"

"But we run it the same."

"Ah," he said. "Just for looks. The boys come in and hang out, and no one is going to say shit about it. We don't have to sneak around. Smart."

"A little discretion would still be good," she said.

He lifted a hand. "I hear you. Yeah. What are you thinking as compensation?"

I slipped off the chair. "I'll let you two talk." To Gillian, I said, "I'll wait for you outside."

***

It took less than thirty minutes for Booster to leave the bar. When he did, I hopped off the tailgate of my truck.

I thought he might walk over and say some words to me, but he didn't. He headed for his Harley, swung a leg over, and started it. Booster merged into westbound traffic without ever looking in my direction.

When Gillian walked out, she found me and smiled. As she neared, she said, "That was fun."

"Did it go okay?"

"As good as could be expected. Last week, I was a lone wolf. This week, I've got two partners. I want to blame you, but it was my own damn fault."

"You didn't have to get into bed with either of them."

She looked both ways in the parking lot. "It was either that or lose the business. A hundred percent of nothing doesn't sound appealing. So, I'm going to take a haircut—a deep one at that. But I've been living too fast and loose for too long. I was bound to get caught. I may hate the situation, but it's probably for the best."

"You're welcome."

A black 1987 Chevrolet Monte Carlo drove toward us. Gillian stepped near me. The Chevy slowed as it neared. Rock sat behind the steering wheel. He rolled down the window. "You okay?" he asked Gillian.

She nodded.

"I'm heading to the clubhouse."

"Be careful," she said. "He wasn't happy that you were there."

"I'll take some shit for it, but everyone has family. We all know the rules."

She jerked her head toward me. "John was explaining the rules earlier."

Rock eyed me. "Yeah? That's good." He reached out and patted her arm. "I'll call you later." He drove away.

Gillian turned to me. "And you're sure there won't be another attack?"

"It's been handled."

"How do I know?

I considered what I could tell her.

If I told her that Double G originated the attacks, that would open a can of worms. Besides, there were already enough people out there who knew what happened—Double G and his crew. The Turk also knew. If any one of them got loose lips and the Wasted Souls found out, blood would be spilled—they'd want revenge for Rock getting shot.

Sure, he'd gotten one of Double G's men with a shotgun, but that likely wouldn't be where they would want the payback to end. They'd take it to Double G, and I'd given the man my word. He would take any attempt on his life as if the words had come from my lips.

So, there was only one thing I could say to Gillian. "You have to trust me."

"This means you found the leak," she said. "Who was it?"

Telling her about Remo wouldn't do any good. If she said anything to Rock, the Souls might start down the path of squeezing him as I did, which would lead to

Trevor Kobold and Yaban Karga. They'd eventually reach Gary Gaspar.

I didn't want to do it, but I repeated my previous answer. "You have to trust me."

"How do I do that?"

"You don't have to pay me."

The words tasted horrible. I wanted the double fee. And I felt I'd set up her business for the future. Yes, she essentially took on new partners and reduced her income because of it, but no one would dare attack her in the future.

"You'd walk away from your fee?" she asked.

"I've got no way to prove what I did. If you don't trust me, don't pay me."

She twisted her lips. "Let me get my purse."

***

That night, I sat on the back steps and drank a beer. I quietly toasted my success. I'd dealt with not only Double G but the Dead Boys and the Wasted Souls, and nobody got seriously hurt. Well, Rock got shot in the shoulder, and one of Double G's hired hands took a shotgun blast to the gut. Who knew what had happened to him?

But I didn't get hurt, and I didn't have to hurt anyone. I had a pocket full of cash to boot.

Corporal sat near me. We watched an old Buick drive slowly through the alley. Its metal creaked and groaned as the car bounced over ruts and potholes. A small plume of dust followed it. When it cleared the alley, the car turned north and sped from the neighborhood. The engine sounded as if one of its cylinders wasn't firing correctly.

Next to my hip, my cell phone rang. I checked the caller screen before answering.

"Hey, there," I said.

"What are you doing?"

"Hanging with the dog. Thinking."

"About?"

"You." It was a lie, but the sort a man tells a woman to lead a conversation where he wants it to go. I imagined her smiling.

Stacy's voice changed. "Want to tell me about it?"

"Not over the phone."

"Oh." Now, I imagined the smile slipping from her face.

"It's not like that," I said.

"What's it like, then?"

"Maybe we can meet tomorrow sometime." I shrugged even though she couldn't see it. "You know, like real people, in the daylight."

"With the kids?" Her voice sounded hopeful.

"If that's what you want, then yes."

"John, that sounds great. Really. Why don't I text you during my lunch hour tomorrow? We can make a plan."

"Doesn't have to be fancy."

"With the kids, it shouldn't be." There was a pause as if she were considering her next words.

I wondered if maybe I should say something.

Finally, she said, "Well, okay. Until tomorrow."

"Right. Sleep well."

"You, too."

The phone call ended.

I stared at the phone and then eyed the dog. "We'll get this figured out."

He flopped to his side and groaned. He'd seen this movie before.

Chapter 16

I arrived at Eight Ball Billiards shortly after they opened. The bartender nodded as I entered, then turned back to cleaning. No one sat at the bar, and no other customers were in the booths.

The pool tables sat silent under the soft glow of hanging lamps.

From overhead, Peter Frampton's "Do You Feel Like We Do?" played softly through the speakers.

Deacon sat in his usual spot. Keith was next to him. Deacon seemed to be speaking intently, and Keith nodded. I waited at the furthest pool table while they finished their interaction. It only took a couple of minutes before Keith stood and headed in my direction. When he neared, the heaviness of their conversation was evident in his eyes.

He said as he passed by, "Go on back."

"How's he doing?"

"Don't ask."

Keith continued walking until he got to the bar. He sat and motioned toward the bartender.

I joined Deacon on the bench. In his hand was his ever-present pool cue. The sickness was easy to spot now that I knew it was there. His eyes appeared sunken and tired. He was unshaven, but that didn't hide the hollowing in his cheeks that had begun to appear.

This morning he wore a new t-shirt—one that correctly fit his now smaller frame. He always looked as if his clothes came from a thrift store, but this one was blue and crisp with the folds still present from when it had sat on a store shelf. Deacon didn't seem to be a man to worry about his appearance. Who might have bought it for him? Had Rosemary Brown as an act of friendship?

"John Cutler," Deacon said. He forced a smile, and his voice sounded as if it was strained this morning. "The word is you've made some new friends."

"Friends would be a stretch. You talked with Tremaine?"

He waggled the pool cue in slow, wide circles. "He also said you two had a conversation. Thank you for that."

"Not sure how much help my words are going to be."

"All we can do is hope. You're helping the Dead Boys, too? Christmas must have come early, considering you're in such a giving mood."

"It was good for everybody."

The arc of the pool cue tightened until it stopped. "Not for the Souls, I hear. You blocked their expansion plans. They must not have welcomed that."

"It wasn't an authorized expansion by the club. One of the members got a little big for his britches."

Deacon cocked his head. "You better hope that member never comes to power."

"I'll deal with it if he does."

"The John Cutler way," Deacon said. "Act now. Pay later."

We sat quietly and listened to John Mellencamp's "Jack and Diane." I wasn't a big rock and roll fan. Most of the rock music I knew was courtesy of my childhood. I moved away from it by the time high school came around. However, it was hard to grow up in the eighties and not like "Jack and Diane."

"You ever have days like that?" Deacon asked.

"The one in the song? High school girlfriends in the backseat of a car?" I shrugged. I didn't want to ask if he had days like that. "You okay?"

He nodded but didn't answer.

The Mellencamp song got to the bridge. It's the part about enjoying youth before we grow into women and men. It was too late for all that now.

"I'm on the Atkins diet," Deacon said. His voice didn't carry much conviction. "You know the one?"

"High protein, low carbs?"

He nodded. "Doing it for my health." He didn't look at me while he lied.

I let it be.

Eventually, the Mellencamp song ended, and a commercial for some heating and air conditioning company started.

"Where's Double G fit into your mess?" Deacon asked.

If I told him, there'd be one more person who knew, but Deacon wasn't a man for retelling another's secrets. "He hired the team that set the whole thing in motion."

"What was Gaspar going to do with a marijuana grow?

"Sell it off," I guessed. "Gaspar's like a shark. He needs to keep moving, or he'll die."

Deacon looked down. "Yeah." He nodded a couple of times and then stood with some effort. That wasn't anything new, though. Deacon's size limited easy movements. "I'm gonna practice now."

"Want to play a couple games?"

"Appreciate the offer, John, but I think I'm just gonna work alone for a bit."

We weren't the type of friends where I could call bullshit on his behavior. We weren't the type of friends where I could say I knew something was happening and offer to help. We weren't the type of friends where I could walk up and put my arm around the man.

We weren't friends at all.

We were business associates.

I stood and left.

***

Remo Lightly showed up at my office around noon. When he appeared at the screen door, I was bent over the newspaper, reading an article about another SPD officer's questionable off-duty behavior.

"Hey," he said. "Can I come in?"

"Yeah."

I hadn't expected to see him. With Gillian's problem wrapped up and her having paid me on the spot, I figured Remo was no longer in the mix of my life.

He entered the house and sat in one of the chairs near the desk. "Thanks for helping Gillian." He didn't sound pleased about it.

"What's wrong?" I closed the paper.

His brow furrowed, and his lower lip jutted out in a pout. "Nothing."

"Remo, you came here for a reason. What's going on?"

He waved a hand. "I gotta work through a middleman again. My cut just got cut."

"I'm sorry to hear that, but what do you want me to do about it?"

"I don't know, man. Tell me how to negotiate with those people."

I crossed my arms over my chest. "For starters, don't refer to them as 'those people.'"

Remo's face pinched. "Ah, man. That's not what I meant. You know that. I meant how can I get them to see that I'm special? That I'm a commodity?"

"I don't think that means what you think it does."

"But you understood it."

I sighed. "Remo, it's the Dead Boys—"

He winced. "That name gives me the willies."

"It's supposed to. Listen. Nothing is going to change. You either accept their terms, or you work elsewhere."

His face brightened. "You think maybe Trevor would take me back?"

"Like a jilted ex-girlfriend? Sure, why not? I don't see how anything could go wrong there."

Remo stood. "Thanks, man. That's what I needed to hear."

"No, Remo. He's not going to take you back. Sit down."

He dropped into his chair.

"You burned that bridge. You wanna burn another one, too?"

"Maybe. I don't know."

"What skills do you have?"

He eyed my desk. "Maybe I could help you around here."

"No."

"Why not?"

"Because you're a thorn in my side."

"Geez, man. That's not nice."

"You either work with the Dead Boys—"

Remo cringed.

"—or you take your skills on the road."

"Like find another dealer?"

"Like leave town. I don't think these guys would be as forgiving as Kobold if you left and kept dealing."

"But I'm too old to start over," he whined.

"Maybe Elva would let you work the bar."

He stood. "I'd rather work for the Dead Boys."

"Then there's your answer."

"Thanks for all your help." His tone dripped with sarcasm.

"You're welcome, Remo."

"You don't have to look so happy about it."

"I consider your misery interest on the fee you withheld from me."

His face flattened. "That's cold, Cutler."

"Gillian said I needed to start charging it."

He pointed at me. "So cold."

"Good luck with the Dead Boys."

Remo spun and shoved the screen door open. "Cold!" he shouted as he walked down my sidewalk.

***

They were already waiting when I arrived at the McDonald's on the South Hill. There were many closer fast-food restaurants, but this was one of the only McDonald's with a PlayPlace.

Two children sat across from Stacy in a booth. Two trays of food sat between them. The kids already had their happy meals opened and were eating. I paused and smiled at the kids before sliding in next to Stacy. She beamed at me and then faced her children. "Kids, this is my friend, John."

The boy eyed me with curiosity, but the little girl grinned back with cheeks stuffed full of food. He had brown hair and glasses. She wore her blond hair in pigtails. The left tail had mostly come free by now. The boy held a French fry covered in mustard. The girl gripped her hamburger with both hands. She'd already eaten half of it.

Children in the PlayPlace shouted with joy as they climbed, slid, and jumped through the various obstacles. A large window allowed the patrons in the restaurant to see what was occurring inside.

"John," Stacy said, "this is Ethan and Hailey."

"How you guys doing?"

The kids didn't say anything but instead returned to eating. Ethan was a dainty eater, carefully swirling a fry through a puddle of mustard before placing it in his mouth. On the other hand, Hailey simply shoved the burger into her mouth like a ravenous tiger.

"They were hungry," Stacy said, "and they want to go play, so we ordered for you. Do you like Big Macs?"

"Who doesn't?"

She handed me a cardboard box. "I figured we could share the fries."

Hailey smiled at us, which reminded me of my daughter at that age.

Ethan refused to make eye contact. He kept his head down and continued his mustard art project.

"And I'm not sure if you drink soda, so I got you a coffee." Stacy handed me a small cup but pulled it back. "Is that okay? Do you drink soda?"

"Coffee's great. No worries."

For ten minutes, the four of us ate and chatted. Ethan contributed the smallest amount of talk—a few yeahs and uh-huhs to the questions I asked. Hailey was far more responsive. Even though I barely understood her words, she prattled happily on.

When the kids reached a point where the PlayPlace was more alluring than the food, they simply stopped eating and stared at their mother. Stacy asked, "Want to go?"

Both kids nodded.

She jerked her head. "All right then."

They slid out and ran toward the door to the PlayPlace.

"What do you think?" she asked.

"They're nice."

Stacy watched her children enter the playground. "Hailey seems to like you."

"She reminds me of Erin at that age."

"Ethan will warm up to you."

"With time."

She put her arm around me. "Does that mean you're willing to try?"

"I'd like that."

"Tomorrow night is Friday."

I raised an eyebrow.

"Why don't you come for dinner?" she asked.

"And stay the night?"

"Well," she bobbled her head. "We still have to be secretive about that. Are you okay with sneaking out before they wake up?"

I'm sure my grin held no secrets. "You're the boss. Whatever you say."

She kissed my cheek. "You say the nicest things, John Cutler."

Did You Enjoy the Book?

Thank you for reading *Cutler's Bargain*. I'm always grateful when a reader takes time out of their day to comment on one of my novels. If you do write a review, please email me, and let me know. I'd love to say thanks!

About the Author

Colin Conway is the creator of the 509 Crime Stories, a series of novels set in Eastern Washington with revolving lead characters. They are standalone tales and can be read in any order.

He also created the Cozy Up series which pushes the envelope of the cozy genre. Libby Klein, author of the Poppy McAllister series, says *Cozy Up to Death* is "Not your grandma's cozy."

Colin co-authored the Charlie-316 series. The first novel in the series, *Charlie-316*, is a political/crime thriller that has been described as "riveting and compulsively readable," "the real deal," and "the ultimate ride-along."

He served in the U.S. Army and later was an officer of the Spokane Police Department. He's owned a laundromat, invested in a bar, and run a karate school. Besides writing crime fiction, he is a commercial real estate broker.

Colin lives with his beautiful girlfriend, three wonderful children, and a codependent Vizsla that rules their world.

Also by Colin Conway

The John Cutler Mysteries

Cutler's Return
Cutler's Chase
Cutler's Friend
Cutler's Cases
Cutler's Bargain

The 509 Crime Stories

The Side Hustle
The Long Cold Winter
The Blind Trust
The Suit
The Value in Our Lies
The Mean Street
Murder by Any Other Name
Black and Blue in the Lilac City
The Only Death That Matters

The Flip-Flop Detective

Strait Over Tackle
Strait to Hell
Strait Out of Nowhere

The Cozy Up Series

Cozy Up to Death
Cozy Up to Murder
Cozy Up to Blood
Cozy Up to Trouble
Cozy Up to Christmas
Cozy Up to Danger

The Charlie-316 Series (with Frank Zafiro)

Charlie-316
Never the Crime
Badge Heavy
Code Four
The Ride-Along

Others

Tales from the Road (with Bill Bancroft)
Some Degree of Murder (with Frank Zafiro)